FOREVER FORTY
A MAGICAL MIDLIFE DEATH NOVEL

TIA DIDMON

Forever Forty

Copyright © 2023 Tia Didmon
All rights reserved. This book or any portion thereof may not be reproduced or used in any manner
whatsoever without the express written consent of the publisher except for the use of brief quotations
in a book review.

This is a work of fiction. Names, characters, businesses, places, events and incidents are either products
of the authors imagination or used in a fictitious manner. Any resemblance to actual persons, living
or deceased, or actual events is purely coincidental.

I love hearing from my readers so please contact me at:
https://tiadidmon.com

Other books in this Series
Forever Forty
Forty Proof and Dead
Forty Shades of Dead
Forty Days and One Vampire Night
Forty Reasons to Die
Forty Deaths till us Part

CHAPTER 1

My business partner gave me a warning look as I listened to the coven representative. Since I was blessed with little magic, I rarely had to deal with the leaders of the magical community. Unfortunately, whatever spell or ritual they were working on required a rare flower, and our shop was the only place in Black Blossom County that could import the rare plant they wanted.

Deanna and I opened Powerful Petals over ten years ago and we made a decent living, though we both had small houses and mortgages to go along with them.

"Raven, are you even listening to me?" Brigid hissed as I grabbed a pad of paper from the counter beside an unfinished bouquet I was working on.

"I am writing it down now. Star canyon is a rare flower and almost impossible to source. If I can get a few seeds, I will be able to induce their growth in the right conditions, but there is no way to procure the amount you are looking for in under two days." I had her order memorized, but she was the kind of person who thought everyone around her was an imbecile except for the current high priestess.

Brigid pointed a perfectly manicured finger at me. The blood-red color matched her couture suit with gold buttons. Coven leaders were always dressed to impress, even when frequenting a lowly flower shop. "You will get my order, Raven; you have done almost nothing for this community. We have had little use for your ability to induce plant growth. It is about time you contributed to the coven. God knows we have supported you this entire time."

I grunted before I could stop myself. Deanna was standing by one of the glass shelving units with various floral arrangements. She appeared to be merchandising the store by adding small figurines and hanging crystals. The large bay windows with the store name printed on top of them created a bright and airy space, allowing the natural light to flood in and illuminate the stunning array of colorful blooms.

"Sure." I couldn't agree with her analogy, as the coven had never done anything for me. While it sponsored witches with powerful magic, it had little use for those of us with minor talents. I had never received a dime from them. My business partner Deanna had abilities more befitting the coven and garnered more respect within the magical community.

Brigid thrummed her fake fingernails on the long wooden counter. It was lined with buckets and vases of fresh-cut flowers, waiting to be arranged into my next creation. "Don't be waspish, Raven. You will get paid handsomely for this order. God knows you could use it. You are behind on your taxes for the plot of land you and Deanna use to grow your local shrubs and flowers."

"Those taxes were due yesterday, and we will have them paid by next week. We are just waiting for payments from a few orders."

Why did the coven always make me feel like I was a

second-class citizen? My mundane family never made me feel like this. I often wished I had no magic at all and hadn't had to grow up in the doctrine of the coven. But if you had any power at all, you were a witch, and nothing could change that.

Brigid touched one of the vases I was working on made of hand-blown glass. The orange color woven in the glass accented the lilies it currently held. "You were fortunate to partner with Deanna. Her ability to manipulate the elements has created some amazing pieces. This store wouldn't survive if you had to purchase most of your products."

It was true that Deanna made the vases for the store, but I grew a lot of what went in them. Anything that could grow in the cool climate of Black Blossom County. But we still got a lot of our supplies from Seattle, which was the closest major city. "Yes, I am lucky to have her." My tone was adversarial as my patience with the second seat of the coven had depleted.

Deanna put a crystal vase down on the shelf a little too hard. "Sorry. I'm clumsy today. Brigid, you know we are happy to have the coven's business. Raven is right. The seed is hard to come by and doesn't grow quickly. Even with her encouragement. We will grow what we have tonight. You know she is stronger at midnight. We will get the order out together as quickly as possible. The coven is always punctual about payment, and we could use that right now."

Brigid glanced at my white apron with a black logo of a rose blossom. We had several variations, but this was my favorite. "Few witches have the restrictions she does. It's inconvenient and quite pathetic, but as long as we receive the order by the end of the week, Ursula will be happy."

The high priestess was never happy, but nobody wanted to see her mad. She was the most powerful coven leader yet, and no witch in their right mind crossed her. I forced myself to smile as Deanna rushed to the door and held it open for Brigid as she left.

Deanna exhaled as she went behind the small counter that held the cash register. "That was fun." She unwrapped her black apron with a white logo. Her tall, slim body looked good in any of our apron colors and her styled red hair was vibrant against her white blouse.

"It always is. I hate coven orders."

Deanna pressed a button on the register, and it chimed when it opened. "Me too, but they pay the best and we do need to pay the taxes on our land." She pulled twenty bucks from the register. "You want dinner. Looks like you will be up late tonight."

"Sure. Get me a roasted chicken salad with light dressing."

Deanna's shoulders sagged. "Are you still on a diet? You have lost over twenty pounds. You look great."

"I need to lose twenty-five more, but Jana is on her way over, so wait and see if she wants anything." My daughter's visits always brightened my day. She was the light of my life, and nothing made me happier than seeing her. I placed another flower in the arrangement I'd been working on when Brigid arrived. "Was that me or was there something up Brigid's ass today?"

The cash register drawer made a loud click as she closed it. "A case of the Twilight Conclave blues, I'm sure."

It was the eve of the Twilight Conclave where all factions were required to meet to discuss any updated protocols and disagreements. The human delegate always acted as an intermediary between the vampire overseer and the witch high priestess. While the leader of the coven was powerful and animated when she didn't get her way, the leader of the vampires was the complete opposite. "I imagine meeting with the vampire overseer is stressful."

Deanna winked at me. "Have you ever seen him?"

I knew what she was getting at. Witches and vampires had gone to war many times in our history and while we had a tentative peace agreement thanks to the mundanes, which both species needed, the vampire leader was next-level attractive. "I saw him once when I was ten. Scary as hell. I don't think he knows how to smile."

"Super sexy though."

"Gross. If you don't mind the fact that he is dead. It would be like sleeping with a corpse."

Deanna rolled her eyes. "Come on, we have a few vampire clients."

I placed a silver spray in the arrangement. "We do?"

She chuckled. "Not really, but if they have money, I would certainly accept it."

The sweet fragrance of the arrangement increased as I turned the vase that contained it. "They have lots, but you will never catch a vampire in a witch-owned store."

Deanna moved to the window. "The sun is going down, so they will be out soon. Speaking of the Twilight Conclave. Is your new main squeeze guarding the new delegate?"

"No. Cameron is part of the Paranormal Special Operations Task Force, but he isn't assigned to the new human delegate. You need to be a senior PSO officer for that. Besides, we aren't at the squeezing part yet, but I hope to be soon. He is sexy." We both laughed as I finished the arrangement.

Deanna stared out the front window before rearranging a few items we had sitting on the shelf in front of it. "How many dates have you been on now?"

"This will be our fifth."

"What does he think about you being a witch?" she asked.

I shrugged. "He knows I have low-level magic, but he is human, so why would he care? Most mundanes don't have an issue with us."

"Have you told him about Isra?" she asked coyly.

I grunted as I put the new arrangement on one of the glass shelves. "By the way, my best friend and baby daddy is a drag queen is not the best conversation starter. That falls under date ten or twelve, don't you think?"

Deanna laughed. "True, but hopefully he is open-minded. Could you imagine having to explain your situation to a vampire?"

"Hardly? They seem to lose their ability to smile when they die. Isra would have a field day with a vampire."

"He would. When is Jana coming?"

"She should be here soon." Deanna didn't have children, though she had been married. I was the opposite.

"That girl has the sunniest disposition I have ever seen. It's a shame she isn't a witch."

This was a debate my business partner and I would never agree on. "Bite your tongue. I am thankful she wasn't burdened by magic. She got to skip the endless days of learning about magic and the atrocities of vampirism."

"I suppose. So, does the fifth date include sex, or am I just being hopeful?"

"Honestly, I have no idea. It has been so long for me. I may need a broom to sweep out the cobwebs first."

Deanna laughed. "How very witchy of you."

I went to the storage room in the back. It was small and consisted of worn metal and wood shelves that held extra supplies and overstock merchandise. But it also had a seed tray that contained the few star canyon seeds we had left. I had never heard of the flower until the coven had asked for it, and dealing with the import of such a rare plant was tedious.

The remaining seeds were in my hand when I returned to the front of the store, and Deanna narrowed her gaze. "Are you going to grow it now? I thought you would wait."

I placed the seeds in a small pot and covered them with soil. "I am just going to warm the earth and add a little water. It will make things easier tonight if they have had some nourishment." I sent a small pulse of power into the soil, but the rude coven member was right. I needed the moon to boost me, or I couldn't induce the plant to blossom.

My smile formed when the door opened, and my daughter walked in. Her long hair was identical to mine, but her tan skin and dark eyes were her father's. Her smile could light a room and often did. At twenty she was the same age as I was when I had her, but unlike me, she was in no rush to find a man. She dated, but her father was beginning to get a reputation for running her potential boyfriends off. Nothing was scarier than a pack of drag queens if they didn't think you were good enough for their baby girl. Isra had a full crew at his club and my daughter worked there.

"Hey, sweetheart. I..." my voice trailed off as an attractive young man entered the shop behind her. His blond hair was perfectly styled though short, and his clothes were high-end and nothing I could afford. His pale blue eyes roamed over the store as if he were looking for something, but I knew that we didn't sell anything for a vampire.

CHAPTER 2

For a moment I thought the young-looking vampire had come in with my daughter, but as she approached us with her easy smile, he moved to the rear of the store where we had a greenery section. This warm humid section of the store had a variety of orchids, and I kept my eye on him as he inspected the flowers.

His features were attractive as all vampires were, but he also displayed the over-pale light-blue eyes with the slight darkness beneath that was indicative of his race. I had never seen a vampire with red eyes and his fangs exposed, but I heard it was pretty scary. There were some experiences that were best left unknown. "May I help you, sir?"

The vampire flicked his hand negligently, but didn't turn toward me. "Just looking for a bouquet for my mother. Give me a moment to decide."

Deanna arched her eyebrow at me. Having just said no vamp would grace our store, I felt like a bit of an idiot, but like my partner had said, their money was as good as ours, and they had a lot more of it. "Sure, take your time. We don't close for another hour."

He moved from the orchids to the section of roses. They were by far our most popular flower and one I could grow myself, so they brought the most profit. They came in a variety of colors, but the vampire seemed intent on the red long-stems.

Deanna waved the twenty bucks she took from the till. "Jana, do you want some dinner? Your mom is having salad, but I am grabbing a cheeseburger. Do you want anything?"

Jana put her hand to her stomach. "I just had some of Dad's Jolof rice. I had to drink a quart of milk after, but it was so good."

"Your grandfather was a bit of a jerk, but he did teach Isra how to cook. I need a half bottle of antacids after I eat with him, though."

"He made Puff Puff too. Those doughnuts are so good. They helped tame the spiciness."

Deanna glanced between us. "You realize you are speaking another language."

"No. Nigerian food is just spicy. Isra's mother was Canadian, so he makes a mean lasagna as well."

Deanna shook her head. "The man that got away."

Jana laughed. "Not really. Mom left him. Not the other way around."

Deanna grabbed her purse from behind the counter. "Really? I just assumed that he left you because he was gay."

I didn't get a chance to respond as the vampire approached the front with a bouquet of a dozen roses in his hand. They were bound together in a clear cellophane wrap with sprigs of baby's breath accenting the crimson color. "I will take these, please."

Deanna waved as she beelined for the front door. I loved my friend and business partner, but she wasn't one for confrontation and no witch wanted to deal with a vampire.

My daughter smiled pleasantly at the vampire, and he smiled back as his eyes roamed over her thin, athletic physique.

He motioned to the store. "This place is nice. I am visiting from out of town. You have an excellent selection."

His being new explained why he didn't realize this was a witch-owned store. I doubted he would have come in otherwise, but he had followed my daughter in, and she was a human without magic. I wasn't sure a vamp could tell the difference between me and a mundane, as my powers were so low, but he should have noticed Deanna's power. "Thank you."

I had to admit I was proud of my store. Deanna had help from the council, as her power was rare, and they wanted to be able to utilize it when necessary. So she had the down payment needed when we wanted to acquire the shop ten years ago. Isra had lent me the money and wouldn't have made me pay it back. But I was adamant about running my business on my own and had paid him back in five years.

The vampire winked at Jana. "You are very attractive. Do you live in town?"

Jana laughed. She grew up with vampires and wasn't afflicted with my prejudices. I was thankful for that, in a way. Everything I knew about the vampires had been from the teachings of the witch coven and had learned the hard way they weren't always honest. "So are you, but then all vamps are sexy, aren't they?"

He chuckled, and I hated it. "I suppose we are. Have you taken the test? You would make a stunning vampire."

"Do not even think about it," I snapped.

Jana sighed. "Don't mind my mother. She is a witch so the chances of my blood being compatible are pretty slim, even though my dad is a mundane."

He arched an eyebrow at me. "One of my friends has a

witch mother and a human father. He was compatible. Most humans have an empowered in their family tree. You never know until you try."

Jana smoothed her long black hair. With her light tan skin, she looked like a goddess, and I could understand the vampire's interest in her. "No thanks. I want to age gracefully and have children one day. They will swarm over my father and steal all his dresses."

"Did you say dresses?" the vampire asked.

"My father is Isra Nasir. He owns Club Spice. If you're open-minded, you should check it out."

I loved that my daughter promoted both her parents' businesses whenever she got the chance. She worked for her father, but she still lived with me. I loved Isra with all my heart and always had. When life broke me. He had picked me up and held my hand. Then gave me the greatest gift life had to offer: our daughter. Our story was unusual, but just as beautiful. There was nothing I wouldn't do for Isra or Jana. They were my family. My life.

The vampire laid the flowers on the counter. "There are some distinct advantages to never aging. I never wanted kids, so that wasn't a deterrent for me."

I huffed. "Yeah, but the drinking of blood thing is a bit of a deterrent. Jana is the kind of person who tries to save a bird with a broken wing."

The vampire's eyes narrowed on me, and I was sure I saw a flicker of red before they returned to their pale blue. "Drinking blood can be quite sensual for a human and a vampire. Most check out the local blood club before they make a decision."

Jana scrunched her nose. "No thanks. That's not for me. I can't even handle a hurt animal. I don't want to see humans getting snacked on. No offense. I don't have anything against vampires."

His eyes roamed over my daughter's form. "That's too bad. I would love to taste you."

I slapped my hand on the counter. "Back off, bloodsucker. This isn't the blood club. My daughter is not on the menu."

The vampire smirked at me and continued to stare at Jana. This was one of the times I wished she didn't take after her father. He was gorgeous, with his tanned skin and dark hair. She had inherited his athletic build and sunny disposition. She even loved men as much as her father did. "You can't blame a guy for asking."

Jana frowned, and I wasn't sure if she was afraid or annoyed by the overly flirtatious vamp. She was used to male attention, though I doubted they got many vampires at the club. "Let me ring up those flowers for you." My daughter knew how to run the till. When she was younger, she had helped at the store. Back when we wanted to limit her exposure to some of Club Spice's activities. She punched the amount into the till, but the vampire seemed to freeze.

"Sure," he said.

"That will be fifty-nine dollars."

The vampire sighed before his arm snaked out and he grabbed the front of my daughter's jumpsuit. The yellow fabric tore as his extended fingernails ripped through it. He yanked her forward as his fangs extended and his eyes lit in crimson fire.

My brain seemed to ignite all at once. There was no way to know if Jana could survive a vampire attack. Humans were thoroughly tested before turning and the process was supposedly painful and rigorous. The number one component was blood compatibility. Vampires were not allowed to go rogue and attack.

Their own people would put them down. Sure, the newly turned could go into a rage. The vampires called it blood madness, and the humans had their PSO forces to combat a rogue if needed. So did the vampires and death dealers were the scariest of the lot. Even the PSO and the witch hunters avoided them.

The witches had their own forces. The witch hunters policed their own, as did every species, but this vampire had been conversational and engaging. There was no way he was newly turned and not aware of what he was doing. He was flat-out about to murder my daughter.

I grabbed the bouquet of roses and swatted him as hard as I could. While some of the roses were de-thorned, the one he chose had nice thick prickles, and he growled and released Jana as he pulled an embedded thorn from his cheek. The torn flesh dripped blood, but began to knit together as he turned to me.

"Run!" I yelled to Jana as I moved around the corner of my counter. I could hear Jana running through the storage area at the back and gave a silent prayer of thanks as the rear door opened.

The vamp was focused on me, which was exactly what I wanted. While there was a chance Jana could survive a vampire attack, it wasn't one I could take. Unfortunately, there was no chance I would. Vampire venom was toxic to the stimulant in a witch's blood that created our magic, and the moment his fangs punctured my skin, I would feel the pain. If he bit me, it was over. Witches didn't turn. They died.

The vampire wiped the blood from his face with the back of his hand. Had he been human, the thorns would have taken his cheek off, but the damage was already healing. "You will regret that, bitch."

"You will not be drinking my daughter. Leave now before the PSO calls your death dealers. I have never met one, but I hear they are not super understanding about vamps who break the rules."

The vampire smiled and his eyes seemed to glow despite the bright store lights. "Cassara is about to have a rude awakening. All the death dealers are, but you won't be around to see it. It all starts with your death." He knew the local death dealer leader. I had heard of her. Everyone had, but nobody in their right mind crossed her.

He moved so fast that I wasn't able to track his movements. He grabbed me by the shoulders and twisted me around before he bent me backward and his hand went around my throat. He was behind me, and I stared at the swinging back door, thankful my daughter had done as I asked her. "Go to hell bloodsucker."

"You first," he whispered before his fangs punctured my neck.

CHAPTER 3

The initial sensation sent a sharp pain rushing through my blood vessels before it turned into a scorching fire. The pressure of his fangs against my neck made it difficult for me to suck in a breath and while I would normally worry about an infection, I wouldn't live long enough to develop one.

I tried to recall my training on how to repel a vampire attack. Witches could recover from the venom provided they didn't die. But that was a long, painful process.

I went limp in his arms as he made gulping noises that echoed in my eardrums. When he was lost in the euphoria of his imminent kill, I used the last of my energy to grab a hanging crystal from a nearby display.

The long shard was beautifully crafted into something close to an icicle, and I thrust it backward into his brain. He screamed but while painful, it wasn't fatal for a vamp.

I staggered forward as my daughter reentered the store, using the door of the storage room. She was talking on the phone and barking orders at someone. "No!" I yelled, but my voice was barely a whisper as I turned to face my attacker.

He pulled the long crystal from his skull and threw the bloody shard on the ground. It shattered on the tile and crimson-laced pieces scattered across the floor and bounced off the shelving units.

Jana's voice was getting louder and moved to stand between me and the vampire. "Just hurry, Dad. She is going to die." Of course, she called Isra. Her father would move heaven and earth to save me, and he had many friends in the PSO. But none of them would get there in time. Of that, I was sure.

The vampire grabbed for me, but I stumbled backward and pushed one of the shelving units toward him. It tipped before he simply smashed his way through it. And flowers, glass, and shrubs rained down like crystal rain as he thwarted my attempts to put everything in the store between us.

My body was getting more and more sluggish with every step, and I knew I was running out of time. It wasn't a surprise that Jana wouldn't leave me. I should have expected her to return, but I needed her to do this for me. I could live with my own death, and I would watch her from the gates of the veil itself if need be, but I couldn't accept hers. "Jana, go outside and wait for your father." I put as much steel into my voice as I could muster.

She hovered at the entrance to the storage room with the cell phone to her ear. "I'm not leaving you!"

"You aren't leaving me, baby. You are just making sure I have backup. Hurry, they will be here soon."

The enraged vampire was focused on me and disregarded our conversation. Maybe my original analysis had been incorrect. He seemed to be suffering from blood loss and stumbled a bit, but perhaps a crystal stake to the brain would do that. He may be temporarily insane due to my attack. I was sure a brain scramble could do that.

It didn't take long for me to run out of shelving and merchandise to use as a barrier. My store looked like a bomb had gone off at its center and my escape route had been effectively cut off. I was trapped in the corner with no way to get to the front door and if I made a play toward the back, then I was putting my daughter at risk. That was something I would never do.

He barely seemed to move before I snapped backward and hit the corner of the shelf so hard that a bone in my back cracked. I crumpled to the floor before he lifted me up as if I were a rag doll. His fingers grasped my long hair roughly before he yanked my head back, exposing my bloody throat. "You are next human," he said to Jana as she watched in horror. His fangs pierced my neck once more and the fiery pain returned.

I locked eyes with my stricken daughter. She was frozen in place and if she didn't get out of the store now, she would be his next meal. "Go get your father. Go now. It's my only hope." I knew what I was doing. I could already feel my heart begin to stutter. Each thick pull of his fangs on my neck brought me closer to death.

She didn't move, and I had to accept that what little magic I possessed would be needed to save her life. Not mine. I focused on her mind. It was a technique I had never truly developed and had used mostly on animals. I swore my daughter and Isra to secrecy, as the coven would have used me to influence those around me had they known.

My magic was draining quickly, and despite this unusual ability, it was not powerful or predictable. Fortunately, I knew my daughter's mind almost as well as my own, and the intricate pathways opened to me as I entered her subconscious. *Go to your father, baby. I have loved you since the moment I first held you and will in this life and all those to come.*

A tear slipped from Jana's eye. "No," she whispered, and her voice held a pain that broke me inside. I would do anything to save her from this, but every daughter had to deal with her parents' death, and it had taken me years to get over mine.

I hadn't counted on her fighting me. As she was one of two people who knew about my minor telepathic power, she knew what I was trying to do. It was a hard thing to pull rank on your child. Especially when she was an adult, but nothing would stop me from saving her. *Walk out that door now!* The command hit her mind like a freight train, and she woodenly turned and walked calmly to the door. It made a loud clicking sound as it closed behind her and I slumped in my killer's arms.

As my strength left me, I recalled the joy my daughter and Isra had brought to my life. When there was nothing left and death was imminent, it was funny how your mind refused to focus on those last moments.

Isra and I had shared custody of my willful and beautiful, mundane daughter. He had taught her about culture and human customs while I had explained my heritage and the diversity of being a witch and a human. Jana had the benefit of both worlds and two parents who loved her beyond anything else.

The last time Isra and I had fought was over Jana's prom dress as he had wanted something off a runway from fashion week and Jana had wanted something couture but reserved. I was fortunate my daughter was more reserved like me, but she adored her drag queen uncles and loved every moment she spent with them at Club Spice.

It was comforting to know that Isra would be there for

Jana when I couldn't be. God, I love my couture-wearing best friend. He had given me everything, despite his preference for men. He would be there for her when she cried, and when she got her heart broken for the first time. When she got married or needed advice. There were so many things I would miss and he would have to be the parent for both of us. In the end, I was thankful for the time I had with them. I just wished I understood why a vampire would incite a war over a lowly witch.

The vampire moaned as his supply began to run out and my eyelids drooped.

"Why?" I whispered. He had to know I was seconds from death. There was no reason to lie to me and though it would not bring any comfort in my last seconds, I needed to understand what I had done to bring down this vampire's wrath on me.

He retracted his fangs, but I hung in his arms as I struggled for breath. I knew what a death rattle sounded like. I had been with my dog, Pretzel, when she was near the end. My parents had been out for dinner when her organs began to fail, and I had put her head in my lap and cried as she began to slip away.

He ran his tongue over my wound, and it began to heal. Vampire venom could also be used as a healing agent, and I could feel the tissues on my neck attempting to attach to one another, but the lack of blood in my body stalled the process. "It wasn't personal, witch. You are just a job and were selected because you have very little value in your community. I have some powerful friends and they needed a diversion. Your death will start a war and we need it to enact change. Consider it a revolution of sorts."

"Revolution..." I whispered as my head lolled on my neck and each breath felt like I had a semi-truck on my chest.

His voice dripped low. "If it is any consolation, your daughter escaped, and I will choose another mundane to snack on. You put up a fight and I do respect that."

He had planned this. Long before he came into my shop, he was going to kill me and my daughter. Why would anyone target witches and mundanes? Did he understand the devastation a war would bring to the entire supernatural community? In an all-out war with the advanced weaponry the mundanes possessed, as well as their superior numbers, it wouldn't be the witches or vampires who won. The lycans had probably thought they could do the same thing right before they were exterminated. My chest collapsed for the last time and refused to suck in the next breath. I choked on the blood in my throat before my heart stopped.

CHAPTER 4

My mouth was so dry I thought I had swallowed sandpaper. Since my mind was sluggish and I felt cold, I assumed that my family had found some way to save me. My eyelids lacked the energy to open, but my nostrils flared, taking in all the surrounding smells.

The combination of antiseptic, formaldehyde, and the faint odor of decomposition mixed, reminding me of the decay that occurs after death.

I remembered the last time I had seen my father. He had lain in the coffin in his best navy-blue suit, surrounded by white satin. He looked perfect and at peace, but when I kissed his forehead, I inhaled the same scent.

There was crying and shouting in the background, but it was from an adjacent room. Was I in a hospital? They didn't use formaldehyde, did they? The answer was yes, but only in the morgue. I wouldn't be taken to a mundane facility. A witch who was attacked by a vampire would be in a private-run clinic, but why were my surroundings so foreign to me? I struggled to open my eyes when my daughter's voice raised above those around her.

"How could you let this happen? You are supposed to protect your people!"

My people would be part of the coven, and I assumed they were here to question me about the attack. I remembered struggling to breathe and the vampire's lilac-scented breath. It had seemed strange, but I guessed that was my blood. I worked with plants and my primary power induced growth and rebirth.

It took all my strength to force my eyes open. The single fluorescent above me was like a floodlight shining directly on my face as my lashes fluttered.

Once my eyes adjusted to the brightness, I tried to move my hand, but my limbs refused to respond, and I glanced down to find I was covered by a single white sheet. It just barely covered my breasts, but I could tell I was naked under the cover and tried to remember who had undressed me. It had to be for medical attention, but I couldn't recall anything after I passed out at the store.

My eyes wandered the room, and I realized why everything was so unfamiliar. I had never been in this room before. The last time I was in this building, I'd been taken to a glass window and the coroner had opened the curtain so I could identify my father's body.

This area was much larger than that small viewing room. It had one wall devoted to refrigerated storage units for holding bodies, as well as several metal tables. All were empty except for the one I was lying on. There was a rolling cart beside me with various tools and equipment for performing autopsies and other postmortem examinations.

I noticed the open door with an adjacent room that was equipped with another table, sinks, hoses, and other tools for cleaning and repairing the bodies. How had they made such a catastrophic mistake? My body felt like it was wrapped in steel chains and refused to move, but I was dead.

I tried to muster my meager ability, but the tiny well of magic that had acted as a safety net was devoid of power. Of life. The vampire must have weakened me to the point of exhaustion and death, but I was still here. I had to find a way to alert my family.

Isra yelled something at whoever they were dealing with in the room down the hall. I had been in that room too when my father had passed, and they needed to confirm who he was. The bus accident had been graphic, and people had been flung in multiple directions, some losing limbs. I had waited in that room for over an hour while families were asked to identify their loved ones. Unlike my mother, Dad had been a mundane, and I had to deal with the human delegate in charge at the time.

The doors that led to the main hall swung open and a man wearing full scrubs, an apron, and a matching cap walked in. He was looking at the chart in his hand and dropped it on the desk in the corner. My eyes followed every action, but I still couldn't move or make a sound.

If this was a nightmare, it was the most vivid and scariest one I had ever had. It was also the most realistic. I smelled his cologne, and he was halfway across the room. Morticians usually went light on the aftershave. He grabbed a sterile mask from the box on the shelf beside his desk before grabbing a pair of blue latex gloves.

Whatever was in that file held his attention as he continued to read it while slipping the string from the mask over his ears and snapping the gloves into place as he donned them.

He approached the table and began setting a few implements from the side counter on the rolling cart beside the long metal table. The top tray was full when he grabbed a scalpel and pressed a finger into my breastbone.

I felt it but still couldn't form words. Why wasn't he looking at me? Surely he could see my eyes were open. They were right? I wasn't a ghost.

The attack at the store was fresh in my mind and I recalled the horrible events blow-by-blow. I focused on my lungs as I remembered fighting for air. The pull of that last breath.

That was when I realized I wasn't breathing. I could hear the mortician inhale and exhale against his mask. A flutter of sound before his heartbeat created a steady staccato of rhythm within the room. Something about that sound made my mouth water, and I tried to focus on pushing air through my lips. Just the smallest of sounds to garner the mortician's attention.

I recalled my coven teachings as a teenager. When an untested human was bitten by a vampire and died from their wounds, they were placed in a holding area for twenty-four hours to see if they turned. It was reported that they were immobile at first and their body didn't bounce back immediately. No witch had ever seen the process, as the body would have been remanded to the local Shadow Bone Clan for verification of death or a turn. Nobody was exactly sure what they did with a fledgling in the first few weeks, but they were only seen in public with a senior until they proved they were not susceptible to blood madness.

But I was a witch; I couldn't be turned into a vampire. I was immediately remanded to the city morgue where the coven leaders would work with the human PSO to determine who killed me and why. Since I died from a vampire attack, the vamps would be under investigation until my murderer was apprehended and my death revealed.

Still, my waking mind went against everything the coven

taught me. I had no doubt that if the vampire overseer believed that witches could turn, he would've had a representative at every empowered attack over the last few hundred years. When a witch died, no vampire came to check if she turned. There was no record of such an occurrence in their long, sordid history. Back when there were four species, humans remained the only common denominator.

Humans could bear empowered children when married to a witch. Humans could be turned into a vampire or a lycan, provided they had the correct bloodline, but witches could not turn into a lycan or a vampire. The lycans had been extinct for a thousand years. Since the last supernatural war, it was reported that vampire blood was toxic to them and lycan blood was just as deadly to vampires.

There were many theories surrounding the war, but only one vampire alive had seen a werewolf, and that was the overseer himself. He would be taking his secrets to the grave, and there were many witches who would love to help him get there.

The mortician grabbed a small tray and placed it on my chest. He angled the scalpel down and the tip bit into my chest. The pain made me gasp, and he dropped the silver blade and backed away.

He snapped the mask from his face with one hand and looked at me in horror. "That's impossible. You are a witch. I saw your birth records."

My lips moved, but no sound escaped.

CHAPTER 5

The mortician looked like he had seen a ghost. With his mask off, I could see his now pale features. He had wisps of sandy blond hair sticking out from under his blue cap and his hazel eyes were wide. He rushed back to his desk, grabbed the file he had placed there, and reopened it quickly.

"There must have been a mistake. You are listed as having low levels of magic. You must have been diagnosed incorrectly. You are a mundane... or were." His name tag read Dr. Johnson, but I'd met him once before seven years ago. He wouldn't remember me from the hundreds of families he was forced to deal with in their darkest hours, but he had been kind when my dad passed and had said his name was Derek.

I forced my lips to move. "No."

He put the file back on his desk and pulled off his latex gloves. They snapped as he pulled them off too quickly and threw them on the chair in front of his desk. "There has to be some explanation. Witches can't turn. You must have been a mundane."

He leaned over his computer and my name popped up on

his screen. He moved to another tab labeled coven members. He scrolled through the information too quickly for me to read, but I was amazed at how much better my eyesight was. Two weeks ago, I had gone to the optometrist to see about glasses and that prescription was still on order. I knew that vampires had enhanced senses, but I couldn't be a vampire. Derek was wrong about me being a mundane. But I wasn't a vampire. I couldn't be. Something had been done to me. It had to be a spell of some kind.

"Spell," I whispered, though my voice sounded like I had been chugging scotch and smoking cigars for the last week.

Derek turned back to me. "You think this is some kind of stasis spell? That you are still alive?"

I tried to nod, but I wasn't sure if my neck actually moved. It may be something else, but there had to be an explanation.

Derek pulled off his cap and ran his hand through his tussled hair. "It is possible you are a victim of some kind of magic I have never encountered. I want to run a couple of tests before I call anyone in. But I have never seen anything like this, and I have been working here for almost twenty years."

"Yes," I rasped.

Derek opened a drawer beside his desk. He pulled out a stethoscope, which was ironic since he normally dealt with the dead. I remembered watching him place it on a young girl whose mother had died the same day my father had. Derek had been kind to her in the waiting room as her father said his final goodbyes to his wife.

I forced air into my lungs. Apparently, I could breathe but it seemed to serve no purpose. The air went in and out, but there was no effect on my body.

Derek noticed my lungs move and placed the earpieces in

his ears before he blew hot air onto the bell. Once warm, he put it on my chest. "Breathe in and out."

I forced the air into my lungs and out, but Derek frowned. "You don't have a heartbeat, Raven."

"Spell," I said again, and my voice was less raspy than it had been before.

Derek pulled the stethoscope from his ears. "I don't think there is any spell that can mimic death, but it could deafen my implements. If you truly believe you are alive, let me perform one more test."

I nodded, and my neck moved this time. My hair slid against the steel table. "Please."

Derek grabbed the scalpel from the rolling cart. "This will sting, but a vampire will heal from any stab wound. Humans bleed profusely from head wounds, but they are relatively minor. I am going to make an incision by your temple."

I wanted to tell the insane mortician to go to hell and find another way, but denial wasn't going to get this issue solved. Derek needed to be on my side when we made the report to the coven and the human delegate. I was attacked by a vampire, and he needed to be brought to justice so the overseer would also be brought into the loop, but I had no desire to speak with him myself. Every witch had a healthy fear of the ancient bloodsucker. "Okay."

Derek put the scalpel under his right forefinger. He placed it gently against my hairline before I felt the sting and a slight pressure. It went away quickly, and I held my non-existent breath as Derek stepped away. He went to the side counter and grabbed a small mirror with a stand. When he returned to the table, he held it above my head, angling it so I could see the wound. "Raven, it healed instantly. You are a vampire."

"No," I whispered.

He put the mirror down on the rolling cart. "I checked

your coven records. While your magic was on the low end, there are several testing records throughout your career. You own the Powerful Petals florist shop. I have bought bouquets from Deanna on several occasions. While I haven't seen you since your father died, Deanna mentioned you induced growth in your plants. I thought it was a mistake. That you were misdiagnosed as a witch, but you weren't. You were a witch and now you are a vampire."

My hand moved, and I brought it to my chest. Lying on a metal table with only a thin sheet was daunting, and I didn't want it falling once I mustered the strength to sit up. "It's a mistake. I can't be a vampire."

Derek placed his hands on his hips. "I share your disbelief. There is no precedence for... this. But I can administer a test that will prove you are a vampire. One we use when we believe a mundane was bitten."

"What test?" I wasn't aware there was anything the humans could do to tell if a human would turn.

Derek went to the tall cabinet in the corner. He opened a drawer and took out a small flashlight. The lens was different from the ones I had at home and the handle sleeker, but I wasn't sure how a light could test me. "This is a high-powered ultraviolet light. Every vampire has venom. Even a fledgling. But most people don't realize that even a dead mundane who doesn't turn is affected. Their skin burns under UV light. If yours does, then you are a vampire."

If I had a heartbeat, it would have stopped right there. All the signs were there, but if he gave me this test and I burned, then life as everyone knew it would change. The truth could set you free, but in my case, it could condemn me to life with my mortal enemy. My mind already went to the series of events that would transpire if my skin smoked beneath that light. I couldn't be forced to live as a monster. Everyone, including a vampire, had a choice.

"Do it," I whispered.

Derek nodded and aimed the UV light at my shoulder. He clicked it on, and the skin burst into flame. I screamed, as it felt like my entire body was encased in molten lava. He flicked it off and grabbed a small towel from the second tray on his rolling cart. He covered the smoking wound quickly as my body shook with silent sobs. "Jesus, I'm sorry. I have never seen anybody have such an adverse effect. Though I haven't had anyone who was bitten survive. Any human who was tested and classed as a vampire prospect goes to the Shadow Bone Clan."

I gasped as the pain subsided and held my arm up so I could inspect the damage. The black mark was already fading away and though it had felt like he had put a laser beam through my flesh, the surface burn turned pink and continued to fade. "This is impossible."

Derek pursed his lips. "I agree, but I have to call the high priestess and the overseer. I don't know what to classify you as right now."

I scrunched the thin sheet to my body and held it as I forced myself to sit up. My movements were jerky, as if my body didn't know how to respond to my commands. Only my fear of falling naked to the floor kept me from embarrassing myself. The mortician had no choice but to call the leader of the witches and the vampires, but they were the last two people in the world I wanted to deal with. "Can't I just go home?"

Derek touched my knee tentatively. "I wish there was something I could say. I have no idea what your evolution will be or if this effect is temporary, but you need guidance and I can't give it to you."

I grunted. Derek really was a kind man. "I know." He was also right. Whatever was going on with me could be temporary. Many fledglings passed in the first few weeks. They turned, but they couldn't make the adjustment and the vampires were forced to put them down. That was a death dealer's primary job.

Derek went to the phone on his desk and hit a number. Ursula's high-pitched voice answered on the first ring. "Is Raven's autopsy complete? Can you confirm she was attacked by a vampire?"

"Hold on Ursula. I prefer to give this report once and answer both yours and Rene's questions." He hit another number and the leader of the vampires answered.

"Dr. Johnson," Rene said.

"Mrs. Kane, Mr. Roth. I have completed my examination of Raven St. Clare. We have had an unusual development."

Ursula huffed. "I don't care about any anomalies in her background. Her father is a mundane and so is her daughter. She barely had enough power to be classified as a witch. I simply want you to confirm for the royal bloodsucker that she was killed by a vampire."

Derek cleared his throat. "She was killed by a vampire, but she did not die."

Ursula sucked in a breath. "I was informed she died. We will fire the paramedic who treated her for this atrocity. I will..."

Rene sighed. "Must you be so dramatic, Ursula? If your witch is alive, you should be happy. This development relieves us of any further unpleasantness."

Derek rubbed his forehead. "You don't understand. Raven did die. She also turned into a vampire."

There was complete silence, and the line wavered with a bit of soft static before Rene spoke.

"Then she was not a witch. I will send a representative to collect my newest fledgling and start the process of her transition."

Ursula hissed. "Raven may have had pathetic levels of power, but I tested her myself. I have seen her induce plant growth, and she had a connection to the moon. We cannot fake such power. She is a witch."

Derek glanced at me. "This is why I am calling you. Technically, she is both. I need clarification on the procedure for her. Where does she belong?"

"There has to be a mistake. Brigid is at the morgue in the reception area, fighting with Rene's clan leader. Have her and Dimitri assess Raven. There must be something else going on."

Rene was silent for a moment. "I concur with Ursula. Have them speak with her. I am on my way to you now. The fledgling is my responsibility. I have claimed her. Make it known." He hung up as Ursula sputtered.

"If Rene is coming there, I am too." She slammed the handset down as my shoulders sagged.

"Is my family here?" I asked.

Derek nodded. "I don't recommend we inform them of this development until the faction leaders decide what to do with you."

"Are you going to inform the human delegate?"

Derek shook his head. "I don't need to. Human is the only thing I can confirm you aren't."

I touched the nape of my neck to find it bare. "Where is my locket? I want it back. Now."

Derek rushed to the white sealed bag on the counter. He opened it and pulled the gold chain with the double-sided locket. "Here. Would you like to get dressed while we wait? I can't leave the room, but I will turn my back so you can dress in privacy."

I slipped the chain over my neck. "It isn't like you haven't seen me naked."

"Raven, I am a doctor and I believed you were a corpse. I treat my... clients with the utmost respect."

My fingers ran over the pendant. "I wasn't suggesting otherwise. I just..."

The door to the examination room slammed open as Brigid entered with a tall man who was obviously a vampire.

I had never met the clan leader of Shadow Bone, but like all vampires, he was good-looking. His black hair was pristine, and his eyes were so dark brown they looked black. His tailored gray suit was perfection, as was his white dress shirt and gray vest. The only splash of color was his red tie, which marked him as a royal in the local clan.

His eyes roamed over me with hatred and disgust, but Brigid's were far more disturbing.

"This is impossible. She isn't dead. You made a mistake, Derek."

Derek folded his arms and while he had been kind to me, he didn't seem to have much respect for the second chair of the coven. "I cut her and did a UV test. Other than being far more sensitive to UV rays than a normal vampire, she is one. I can't, however, confirm she was diagnosed as a witch properly. She may have been a mundane all along. If I have to make a recommendation, I will side with the vampires and say she was never a witch."

Dimitri's lip twitched. "This is likely what happened. Vampire venom is toxic to witches. If there were a way to counteract this effect, it would have been discovered centuries ago. Many witches have died in past wars. There has never been a successful turn."

Derek nodded. "That raises my second question. It is too soon to call her turn successful."

Dimitri smoothed his red tie. "That is true. Fledglings are assessed and assigned a mentor for a year or two. They are never in public without one in the first few weeks. We are serious about public safety."

Brigid huffed. "You are an arrogant pig who likes to control your people like cattle. You treat the humans in much the same way."

Dimitri's lip curled to reveal his fangs. He had extended them on Brigid's behalf. "Come now, Brigid. I am more than happy to explain vampire life and the advantages of donating blood to our cause. It is quite enjoyable."

Brigid looked like she was about to be sick, but the static charge in the air alerted me she had placed a protection barrier around her body. The second in the coven was almost as powerful as the high priestess herself, and if Dimitri made the wrong move, he could lose a limb.

Derek held his hands up. "Stop it. Both of you. This is a sanctioned space by all factions. Any physical disagreement in this room will be considered an act of war."

Dimitri's fangs retracted slowly. "My apologies Derek. We have nothing but respect for the humans and their delegate."

Brigid huffed. "Because you need them."

Dimitri smiled at the witch. "As do you." My head hung as we waited in silence.

"Let me through!" Ursula's high-pitched voice penetrated the room before she entered.

CHAPTER 6

The door slammed loudly behind the high priestess. She was wearing a black silk robe that signified she had been in some form of meeting or ritual when Derek called her. She hadn't bothered to change, as she likely wanted to arrive before Rene. The overseer traveled between his many clans, but his local mansion was farther from town than the coven retreat.

Her gray hair was perfectly pinned back, and her makeup was pristine. Her light-green eyes were unusual and had been extremely beautiful when she was younger. The wrinkles at her temple didn't detract from her beauty, but the thin line of her angry lips did. "Prove she is a vampire."

Dimitri moved between me and the high priestess. "Rene is on his way. Since she has no heartbeat and is sitting up and quite mobile for this early in a turn, I think it's safe to say she is one of us. But nothing will be done until he arrives. He took responsibility for her."

Ursula crossed her arms. "Raven, can you tell me about the attack? Did you recognize the vampire who attacked you?"

I crossed both arms over my chest. I felt naked despite the sheet I clung to. "No. He said he was from out of town and wanted flowers for his mother. He wasn't wearing Shadow Bone colors, but he was conversational and flirted with my daughter before he attacked."

Ursula arched an eyebrow. "So, in your opinion, he was not suffering from blood madness. He made a conscious choice to attack you."

I nodded. That bastard had robbed me of my life and now I was stuck with a fate worse than if I had died. No witch would wish this on the worst of enemies. "I just want to go home."

Dimitri cocked his head to the side. "That is the one thing you cannot do. Regardless of your origins, you are a vampire. Sending you to your human family would be unconscionable. We do not put humans in danger."

My eyes snapped to his and while his words seemed noble, his eyes held no compassion. "I would rather die than..."

Rene strode into the room as if he owned it. His pale blue eyes moved immediately to me and roamed over the sheet I clutched to my body.

The ancient vampire had subtle wisps of blond that highlighted his mahogany hair. As if the gorgeous undead leader needed anything to enhance his stunning good looks. Men were supposed to be handsome, but Rene defied a description so mundane. His skin was pale, but not like those of his brethren. He seemed to retain a hint of color his underlings were denied. His suit was similar to Dimitri's but completely black, as was his tie. He belonged to no clan. They all deferred to him. While he was in Black Blossom County, he would reside at the Shadow Bone mansion, but he traveled often for the various conclaves he was forced to attend.

He was accompanied by a death dealer. Not just anyone but their leader. Anybody in their right mind feared Cassara James and the squad of vampires she led. She was wearing a one-piece leather suit that had a slick quality, making it appear wet. But the loops at her belt with multiple weapons attached left no doubt what she was and what she was willing to do to protect the man she accompanied. Her black pixie-cut hair was stylish and added to her deadly appearance.

I wasn't sure if I should laugh or cry. The fact they considered me a threat was ludicrous. Every faction had a hit squad to deal with their criminals. For witches and vampires, that disorderly conduct ended in death. Humans were more lenient with their criminals, but not if they messed with the conclave accords. Nobody could afford a supernatural war.

My arm tightened on the sheet surrounding me when my nipples peaked. It had to be the cool air that was indigenous to the morgue. It couldn't be the sexy vampire leader. While my eyes were basking in his loveliness, my mind wanted to grab the closest scalpel and stab him in the throat. No, it wouldn't kill him, but it would sting a bit.

I shivered when he stepped closer to me. He inspected me like I was a science experiment and with just as much emotion. Still, he was potent, and I had to bite my tongue until it bled to deter my inner vamp vixen. Sure, he was sexy as hell, but he hadn't said a word, and his eyes held the emotion of an anaconda. There was no doubt in my mind, which was deadlier.

My throat seemed to close, and I coughed up dry air. I struggled to swallow, but I didn't seem to possess saliva. It was as if my entire body was working against me.

"You need to feed fledgling," he said in a melodic voice.

My eyes snapped to his. "My name is Raven, and I will decide what is best for me."

Dimitri hissed, but the death dealer's lip twitched.

Rene stepped closer, and I forced myself to remain calm. Just the hint of sandalwood and maple hit my nostrils before I stopped breathing. He held my gaze for a few seconds. "You will do as I ask."

"Get over yourself," I snapped as Cassara coughed, but I could see she hid a smile. Dimitri looked like he wanted to kill me on the spot, and both Ursula and Brigid sneered at the vampire leader.

Rene searched my eyes as if looking for something. "You do not feel the need to obey me?"

"Why would I? Do you think you get a pass for being hot or something? I'm a witch, not a bimbo."

Cassara openly laughed. "Looks like you got a live wire, Rene. Have fun with this one."

Rene glanced at his death dealer comrade. "I'm sure you will. You will mentor her."

Dimitri huffed. "You should have kept your mouth shut, Cassara. Relegated to mentorship is hardly befitting the leader of the dealers."

Cassara flipped Dimitri the bird. "And yet I would rather mentor a witch than spend five minutes alone with you," she said in an overly sweet voice.

Dimitri looked like he wanted to say more, but Rene flicked his hand in the air. "Enough. You are both acting like children. Cassara is young by our standards, but you should know better than to let her bait you, Dimitri."

The high priestess and her second remained quiet throughout the vampire byplay, but they were very interested in the animosity between Cassara and Dimitri. "We need to decide what to do with Raven. There is no proof..."

I was so busy trying not to breathe so close to the vampire overseer, that I failed to notice the threat that the sandpaper feeling in my throat was causing. The room turned red and all I could focus on was the thrum of heartbeats in the room. I could see the pulse of blood beneath Derek's neck and moved to get closer to the sweet smell.

Rene pinned me against the metal table and the sheet slipped down slightly as my breasts smashed against his suit jacket. Part of me knew I should be embarrassed. As soon as he moved, I would be the next contestant at the titty convention, but the haze in my mind refused to recede. I needed that sweet smell. The thirst in my throat was turning the tissue to gravel.

Ursula and Brigid backed away, as did Derek. Nobody was stupid enough to get near a hungry vampire and as a fledgling that had not been introduced to the vampire world, I was afforded certain liberties. I couldn't kill, but vamping out was expected.

Rene held me against him with no emotion and zero effort. I was using every ounce of strength I had, but apparently, that was like a baby bird next to him. "You will feed on me until we can induct you into our ways."

My jaw dropped as a lancing pain pierced my stomach. I expected vampires got hungry, but I had no idea the pain they experienced when they ignored that hunger. My insides were being stabbed with hot pokers and twisting my intestines into knots. "I would rather die," I choked out.

"That can be arranged," Rene said with the same lack of emotion.

Cassara whistled. "Wow, that is some next-level defiance, for a fledgling."

Rene held me immobile, but turned to Derek. "Do you have any blood?"

Derek glanced through the door that led to the adjacent room. "Nothing less than four hours old. Will that suffice?"

"No, I am afraid not. She requires more robust sustenance. Cassara, grab a bottle of wine from my private reserve," Rene said.

I wanted to be mortified, but I was trying not to take the overseer up on his offer. His neck was right in front of me, and I was losing my battle not to inhale. Instinct was a bitch, and I very much wanted to smell his unique and engaging scent. But I kept my eyes locked with the sexy overseer as Cassara slipped from the room silently. She returned in just a few seconds, and I had to wonder how she had retrieved it so quickly. She popped off the cork and passed it to Rene. He put the bottle to my lips and tipped it.

I had no idea what kind of wine this was, but it tasted like heaven had grown the grapes. I leaned against him as I swallowed gulp after gulp of the sweet liquid. It wasn't until Brigid made a gagging sound that I realized some had dripped from my lips to my cheek. Rene pulled the bottle from my lips as I wiped the excess from my skin with the back of my hand. I stared in horror at the blood on my thumb. "No."

Dimitri smiled like a viper. "Rene's private stash is quite rare. You should be honored."

I put my hand to my mouth as I tried to stay my gag reflex. "Oh, god."

"God can't help you, witch," Dimitri said.

I shook my head. "That wasn't blood. It tasted like..."

Cassara sighed. "Trust me, honey. That is blood. If you use your other senses, you can even detect what the human had for lunch before he donated."

My senses flared out before I could stop them. The scent of blueberry and vanilla tickled my nose before my lip quivered. There was no denying what I had just consumed. The death dealer hadn't lied. I was a blood drinker.

I grabbed the bottle and smashed it against the table Rene had me pinned against. Green glass skittered across the metal as the blood splattered on the stainless steel and dripped to the floor as I hissed at Rene.

Cassara pulled a silver baton from her belt, and, in seconds, it extended from both sides and formed a spear at one end. "Drop it, fledgling, or I will end you after I teach you the difference between dissection and death."

CHAPTER 7

*R*ene calmly took the broken wine bottle stem from my hand. "There is no need for threats, Cassara. She is newly turned, disoriented, and hungry. You remember what that was like."

I forced my body to calm, but it wasn't easy with the scent of the vampire leader so close. While his suit was pristine and likely cost more than my car, his body was pressed against mine and was like granite. He died with an athletic body, and it reminded me I would never lose those last twenty pounds I wanted to. Vampires didn't change. I was stuck in pre-menopause chubbiness for life. I made a second attempt to grab the bottle from Rene's hands, and he simply lifted it above my head. At over six feet tall, he towered over me.

Cassara gave a curt nod before she clicked a button on her spear, and it retracted into the short staff she clipped to her belt. "Of course, Overseer." Her eyes remained distrustful, and her hand closed on the silver staff.

Dimitri grunted. "I am not sure it was in our best interest not to kill her. If either species believes that she was a witch and turned successfully, we could have an uprising in both the coven and the clans."

I turned to Dimitri as the haze in my mind subsided. I was still thirsty, but I slipped my hand between mine and Rene's body and grasped the sheet. He moved away enough that I could pull it up over my breasts. "What a shock. A vampire who wants to kill a witch. Go ahead. Maybe my death will inspire my coven to wipe your ass out. Then I wouldn't have to worry about my daughter suffering the same fate."

Dimitri growled as his eyes flickered with red. "You disgusting wench. I will..."

Ursula grunted, but I saw the twinkle in her eyes. "This has been highly entertaining, but I must insist that Raven returns to the coven. If nothing else, she will make a great pet."

I glanced down at the thought of being the coven's personal whipping vampire. It would be worse than anything I could imagine, and I would rather die. My family was already mourning me, so I had to make this decision quickly. I wished I could thank the mortician for making me wait for the meeting between faction heads. "Blow me, Ursula."

Cassara grunted and pursed her lips as the high priestess looked at me in shock. "I beg your pardon?"

I narrowed my eyes at her. "You are old, not stupid. I have no intention of being your test subject. Everyone in the coven knows you would love to get your hands on a vampire. The experiments would be worse than death."

Cassara cocked her head to the side as she stared at the high priestess. "Is that right? And here I thought we could all be friends." Her tone was so cold I shivered. Dimitri's lip twitched, and it was obvious he was enjoying the death dealer's icy stare.

Ursula cleared her throat. "That is untrue. We simply want what is best for Raven."

I wrapped the sheet around me like a toga and secured it by tucking the corner between my breasts. I looked like I was freestyling at a frat party, but if I was going to die in this sheet, I was going to own it. Isra had taught me that. It wasn't so much what you wore, but how you wore it.

Rene glanced at the high priestess. "While we have no proof she was ever a witch, it is obvious she is a vampire. It is unsafe to leave her in human hands, whether they are empowered or not. You and your coven are a food source for her. She needs time to acclimate. To curb her appetite and learn our ways. She is too volatile in her present state. All newly turned are."

Ursula pointed at Rene. "She may be a vampire, but she was a witch. I have several witnesses who will verify she has performed magic. We all need to know how this transpired. Your clan leader is correct in his assumption. This news could be devastating to both witches and vampires alike."

Rene shrugged casually, as if he couldn't care less what my past was or the consequences of my reveal party.

I secured my toga with one hand and moved away from Rene. For a moment, I wasn't sure he was going to let me go. He didn't move, but he gave the impression of a caged tiger, only we were all in the cage with him. I had always feared the high priestess' power, but she seemed like a rabbit in the fox's den next to Rene. Nobody was sure of his powers, as he was the oldest living creature. "You can both stop talking like I'm not even here. I will break this down for you nice and slow, so you both understand. I was a witch but haven't participated in coven business since I turned twenty. My magic was deemed too... What was the word you used, Ursula? Ah yes. Pathetic. Yes, always a nice thing to say to an aspiring witch who looked up to you growing up." I turned to Rene. "I grew up in the coven and actually respected her at one time. As for you. I'd rather shit glass than be a vampire."

Rene shifted his feet slightly, but everyone in the room held their breath. "You no longer possess such bodily functions."

I straightened my shoulders. I knew I was close to death. Not because my body had died a few hours ago, but I had effectively pissed off my former high priestess and the overseer would have no choice but to kill me. Disrespect wasn't tolerated in the vampire community, or so I was told. I wasn't sure what was true about vampire clan life, but I was sure a hierarchy had to be maintained. "I guess vampires lose their wits as they age."

"You have a choice, Raven. You must follow our rules or die."

"I think I would rather die."

Rene assessed me, and there was a faint flicker of red. It disappeared so quickly I thought I imagined it. Maybe it was anger, but he didn't seem to care enough for that. A viper had more personality than he did. "You are already dead. Perhaps you misunderstood my question. What do you want?"

I stared at the floor. It was humbling to know that your bravado was wasted on someone who couldn't care less if I lived, died, or grabbed a yogurt from the fridge. The overseer lived a life of simple disinterest, and that was more frightening than anything. "I want to find out who killed me and why. I also want my daughter protected. He told me he had planned to kill her."

Ursula sucked in a breath, and I knew why she was frightened and mad. A three-way war ended one way. Death to vamps and witches. They were incapable of uniting, even to save themselves in a war against humans. "The vampire attacked your daughter? This was never brought to my attention."

I huffed. "It's not like you would talk to a lowly mundane. She has nothing to offer you."

Ursula smoothed the form of her robe with her hand. "The human delegate will be informed of this development. If vampires plan to prey on witches and humans we must band together to..."

Cassara stepped toward Ursula. "You would like that, wouldn't you? If Raven hadn't turned, we wouldn't have known this was a planned attack. That someone wants dissension between the vampires and the witches. If a vamp has been coerced to go against his clan and kill witches and humans, it will give you the perfect opportunity to discredit us and convince the conclave we had broken the treaty."

Brigid stepped closer to Ursula. Her black dress was plain, but its style left no doubt she was a member of the coven and in high standing. "Do not speak to the high priestess so. This rogue vampire is your problem. Not ours. His motivations are irrelevant. He killed a witch and would have killed a human."

Cassara turned to Derek. "You will report all that has transpired here, including that last statement to the human delegate, correct?"

Derek nodded. "Of course, Cass. It is my job to relay all the information to Mr. Francis."

I was surprised that Derek called her Cass. It was an endearment, and I assumed they must work together a lot. How many people had he been required to contact her for? Some attacks weren't vampire, but she would be informed if it was suspected. And a human could turn. Brigid went pale as Ursula gave her a dirty look. Her outburst had effectively removed any doubt where the coven stood on vampires and her willingness to throw them under the bus would be reported to William Francis. The new human delegate.

I had really liked his wife. She had been one of my best customers for years. I had cried in the backroom when he had come in to order her favorite flowers for her funeral. He was a nice, albeit gruff man, who had served his country and community. He had deserved to spend his elderly years with his wife; instead, he was serving the PSO and leading the Twilight Conclave. Fate had a wicked sense of morality.

Rene ran his hand through his hair. I doubted it was vanity. More likely, the air conditioner had blown a strand in his eyes. "Tell us more about the attack and what the vampire said to you. Was there anything more than death threats? About this war or revolution."

I swallowed hard and glanced at Cassara. "He said Cassara was about to have a rude awakening. That all the death dealers are, but I wouldn't be around to see it. It all starts with my death."

Ursula snorted. "You lie. No vampire would threaten the death dealers. They are feared by their kind. Hell, they are feared by everyone. Why target them?"

Rene turned to stare at the high priestess. "Killing Cassara would hurt the Shadow Bone Clan and suggest weakness in my ability to protect my people. It would also disrupt the death dealers until a new squad leader was chosen. The plan is sound, but unlikely. Her skills are beyond that of any other, including the other Shadow Clans."

Ursula narrowed her eyes at Rene. "You are assuming Raven's attacker told her the truth. A vampire may tell his own the truth, but he can be trusted to lie to a witch or human."

Rene seemed to consider her words, though no emotion showed on his face. He could be considering killing the high priestess or a new paint color for his mansion. It could go either way with the overseer.

As I considered the implication of a conspiracy to start a war, I realized that it was also my daughter's life. Isra's life was in jeopardy. Every human was at risk if the accords were breached. While it was unanimously believed that the humans would ultimately win such a war, there would be massive casualties to those without military training. My daughter was too young, and my drag queen bestie and baby daddy could put a Versace model to shame when he was in full dress, but if you gave him a gun, he would be dead before he figured out how to get the safety off. I turned to Rene. "If I go with you, will you ensure my family's safety? Both Jana and Isra?"

Ursula stepped forward. "No witch would touch a mundane. Your family does not need protection."

I grunted. "You assume I meant just from the witches? I don't. That vampire wasn't the mastermind behind my attack, but he did say I was weak in my community. That I lived a pretty mundane life, so how would a vampire know that?"

Rene stared at me for some time. "A new vampire's human family is always protected. And mundane safety, in general, is my top priority. It is the reason I founded the death dealers."

I couldn't tell if he was lying, but Cassara nodded as if agreeing with him. Dimitri looked pissed, and it was obvious he didn't like the influence Cassara had with the overseer. He would never say anything, though. Every faction was aware of what happened to a vamp that got overzealous in a blood club. "Okay. Derek, will you inform my family about what happened? I need a day or two before I face them. For safety reasons."

Derek pursed his lips. "You are extraordinarily composed for a fledgling."

I laughed without humor. "You think so? I vamped out and wanted to carve Rene a new asshole. I'm not sure composed is the word I would choose."

Derek tried not to smile. "Rene has that effect on people. Or so I am told."

Cass winked at Derek, and I wondered at the camaraderie. Dimitri looked fouler than ever as Rene put his hand gently on my shoulder.

"Come. It's time to see your new home."

CHAPTER 8

*D*erek was kind enough to hold the door to the examination room open for me. He motioned for me to go down the hallway that led to the side entrance. The laneway the coroner's van used to bring the bodies into and out of the building. I kept my head down and focused on keeping my makeshift toga secured in the front while using my other hand to lift the sheet above my feet. Nobody had offered to let me change, but Derek had handed the white bag with my clothes in it to Cassara as she passed him.

I froze when Rene pulled me to a stop by slipping his arm around my waist as I reached for the door handle. "Allow Cassara to open the umbrella. The vehicle is parked in the shade, but your skin is far more sensitive than ours."

I dropped the sheet, so it covered my bare feet and casually removed his arm from my waist. "Yeah. Bursting into a giant fireball is so last year."

Cassara chuckled as she grabbed the long black umbrella propped against the door. She had likely set it there when they came in. I glanced back as Dimitri joined us.

"I will return to my vehicle. My driver is parked in front of you."

Rene nodded and Dimitri exited the building. He didn't bother with an umbrella and was obviously old enough to withstand the shade for a few seconds. I wasn't up on vampire UV tolerance, but assumed it was an age thing.

Cassara opened the umbrella and handed it to Rene before donning her sunglasses. They were a unique design and curved around the sides of her face. There was no doubt those had full UV protection and her suit likely had similar protection. When she slipped on a black leather cap made of the same material as her suit and zipped up the front so her neck and chest were completely covered, I was sure my assumption was correct. She opened the door and held it for Rene.

He put his hand on the small of my back. "Stay under the umbrella until we reach the limo."

I tried not to focus on his hand. He seemed oblivious to his innate charm and lack of personal space. He had seen thousands of vampires come and go. I was just the latest of undead underlings, but my origins were unique. Maybe Rene appreciated a mystery. God knows he didn't seem interested in much.

As we exited the building, he pulled me closer to his body. I knew it was to ensure the filtered light didn't get to me and the sun was moving over the front of the limousine's hood as Cassara opened the back door so we could enter. I pulled my toga up as I sat down and moved to the farthest seat. Rene sat beside me and while he wasn't touching me, I wished he would move closer to the other side.

Cass took the seat opposite me, but her eyes continued to move to Rene. "You're hovering. You never do that."

Rene glanced at her. "I do not hover. I don't fly."

"Don't be an ass. You know what I mean," she said.

My eyes moved around the interior of the vehicle to stop from smiling. Cassara was the one person who was defiant with Rene. There was a story there, and I found myself curious as I inspected my surroundings.

The soft, high-quality leather seats were comfortable and obviously made of premium materials. The accents were glossed wood with a brass finish. The seats were facing each other in a row and there was a mini-bar between them, with a mini fridge. I assumed that was where he kept his stash of premium wine. I wasn't ready to call it what it was. The mood lighting was set low, and the music station was set to soft jazz. I noticed the flip-down TV above the bar, but doubted the overseer had a favorite show.

I had only been in a limousine once and that was because Isra had rented it for Mother's Day and sent Jana and me on a spa excursion. Everyone always wondered why I didn't marry after my fiancé died, but they didn't understand I had everything I needed. Well, I did when I was alive. Now my favorite beach vacation would give me more than a blister.

My memories strayed to my last family trip. Isra always came with us, and Jana would joke she had the coolest and most loving non-coupled parents. Isra had always been a cuddler and that hadn't changed in all the years we had known one another. He held my hand and even his boyfriends over the years had come to accept that nobody could come between us. I must have lost myself in my memories, as Rene said my name.

"What?" I asked.

He looked down at me and I found I didn't like feeling like a dwarf. I wished I had a few more inches on me. Cassara was only a few inches shy of six feet and could have been a model. I had no idea how old she was when she turned but she looked to be in her late twenties while Rene looked to be mid to high thirties. It was so hard to tell with vamps, but the witches were sure Rene was well over a thousand years old and he was the overseer when the oldest scrolls were written. "You didn't answer my question."

I had no idea what he had said to me, but Isra had always said when in doubt, to ask a question. "Did you mean what you said?"

"I said many things. To which do you refer?"

"About mundane safety being your first priority," I said.

He stared at me for several seconds and I wished he would tell the driver to go. "It has always been my first priority... until now."

I wasn't sure what he meant. Did he think a turned witch was some kind of dark omen, or was he concerned about a larger conspiracy? I nibbled my lip, then touched it with my fingers when I realized my fangs were partially exposed. Should I be embarrassed? Did this mean I was hungry again or did I just lack control over my blood juicers?

The leather crunched as Rene shifted in his seat and crossed his legs. "Cassara, since you will be mentoring Raven, you will also ensure her safety. Assign some of your conscripts to Raven's family. We must ensure their safety as well."

Cassara's jaw dropped slightly, and her eyes went to me. "Of course, Rene," she said in a soft voice. I didn't like her capitulation. While I enjoyed her brashness with Rene, I realized there was something unusual about his request. He had already said he would protect my family and help me assimilate so I couldn't discern the nature of Cassara's abrupt turn of emotions. She was curious about me and... hopeful. How did I know what she was feeling? Shit.

Cassara knocked on the partition of dark glass before it

rolled down. "Edward I think we are ready to go, can you..." She stopped when there was a loud thud against the glass window of Rene's door.

"Open up Rene!" Ursula demanded.

Rene calmly cracked the limousine door open and Cassara hissed as she moved away from the light. With his legs crossed, his ankle was exposed to the light and while the thin black socks covered his skin, they were not thick enough to provide full coverage. The wisp of smoke rose above his Italian leather shoes as he regarded the high priestess. "Ursula. What do you want?"

Ursula stared at his smoking ankle and cleared her throat before pointing at me. "She is an abomination. The person we knew as Raven is gone."

"That is not how it works, Ursula, but your ignorance is not my problem. She is a vampire, and you have no purview over her. Would you wish me to dictate to your witches.?"

"Don't be ridiculous," she snapped.

"Then move aside and allow us to leave."

Ursula clutched her robes together as they pooled in front of her in her hunched-over position. She met my gaze. "Please understand. You can't be allowed to live. We made a holy vow to uphold our coven principles. If any piece of you still exists, you will understand the threat you pose. You took the witch's creed. You must..."

I leaned toward her, but Rene put his arm out to stop me from entering the sunlight. "Don't you dare recite the witches' code to me! I believed all that crap until I needed actual help, and you told me to suck it up. That being a witch wasn't all sunshine and roses. You remember that right, Ursula. When I was broken and instead of helping me, you stomped on me like I was yesterday's garbage."

Ursula's hand fisted in her silk robe. "I am not responsible for his death."

"I never said you were, but anyone else would have had some compassion and given me a break from coven duties. You did nothing but laugh when I struggled."

"Everyone experiences loss. It is not my fault you were weak," she said.

I laughed. "Look who is the weak one now. I know your doctrine well. I grew up with it. Trust me that this is a lot harder for me than it is for you. I have to live this nightmare. You just have to return to your cozy villa surrounded by ten acres of perfection, while the vamps stare at me like I'm a leper. Don't worry; I'm sure another vamp will get me when Rene is otherwise occupied. He has thousands of vampires to look out for. He doesn't have time for one errant witch. Hell. You may get lucky, and he kills me himself. God knows he looks like he wants to."

Ursula glanced at Rene, but his expression hadn't changed, though the smell of sizzling flesh began to permeate the air and I wondered if he even felt pain anymore.

He sighed, but now that I was a vampire, I knew he did it for effect. I hadn't seen him take air into his lungs once since he walked into the morgue. Man, if that was what awaited me in immortality, I wanted no part of it. Would I look at my daughter that way? With those same dead eyes? I would rather die now than put her through that.

Rene leaned over without another word and slammed the door in Ursula's face. I smirked because the high priestess was unused to being disrespected, but he rolled down the window when she banged on it again.

"How dare you, Rene?"

"We are leaving, Ursula. The conclave is tomorrow night.

We can discuss all matters up for debate then. It is the reason it exists, after all."

She pointed at me. "She can't be allowed in public."

"It is my responsibility to train her, since her sire is a rogue. If she becomes unstable, I will kill her myself. That is our custom."

Ursula smiled coyly. "I am aware of your position on rogue vampires. But she is not just any vampire."

I felt a tingle in my chest and grabbed my locket with one hand. My eyes darted around the limo, trying to discern what was causing the strange feeling. It felt like energy was being sucked from the surrounding air, but neither Cassara nor Rene seemed aware of the odd sensation. My eyes snapped to Ursula as she continued to debate my future with Rene. I had to give the overseer props. He was not one to bow down to anyone's demands, and while that would likely bite me in the ass later, I was enjoying the high priestess' attempts to manipulate him.

Still, she was doing something. I wasn't sure why I could sense her gathering her magic, but it was likely a residue of my power. Maybe it took time for the component in a witch's blood to dissipate. That same additive that was supposed to kill me rather than allow me to turn.

Ursula shook her head. "I don't think you understand the gravity of the situation." Whatever she was doing, her power was growing.

CHAPTER 9

I had no desire to get closer to Rene, but the hairs on my skin were beginning to rise as if I were close to an electric current. My voice dropped to barely a whisper. "She is up to something."

Rene moved so slowly that I doubted the high priestess noticed. He angled his body to block most of mine from Ursula's view.

"You aren't listening to me, Raven," Ursula said.

"You haven't said anything relevant. I never pretended to be anything more than a low-level witch, but I always helped those around me, including the coven, when asked."

Ursula's eyes twinkled. "With the exception of accelerating some plant growth, you were in no position to help the coven. You forget what happened when you attempted to heal Andre's broken leg when he fell from a tree?"

"I haven't forgotten anything. The bone shifted out of position and I made the wound worse, but I was twelve years old and there were no adults around. I was trying to help."

Ursula's fingers curled over the partially raised glass window. "You are always trying to help, but your intentions and your magic never measured up."

"And this is why we never got along. All you care about is power and privilege. The actual members of your coven are nothing to you unless you can use them."

"Even in the wild, the weak are culled. Do the right thing, Raven. Return to the coven and submit to testing."

I leaned back against the far door, putting as much distance between me and the high priestess as possible. "I'd rather be a vampire." It was the last thing I thought I'd ever say, but it was the truth. I would rather be dead than a coven pincushion.

Ursula smiled as the static in the air increased. "I had a feeling you'd say that."

The spell snapped like a rubber band, but I knew neither Cassara nor Rene could feel it. The fireball formed outside the window as Cassara grabbed for her silver staff. She wouldn't have time to pull her weapon and stab the coven leader through the heart. Once a spell was unleashed, it would complete its instructions. As the flames increased, I realized she had been sucking the heat from the surrounding air and simmering it in a cauldron of her power before releasing it.

When the ball of flame arced toward the open window, something inside me snapped. This wasn't the gentle stream of nurturing power I used to induce a seed to sprout or a small plant to extend its tiny leaves. This power ignited from my soul and formed a lightning shield that arced around the rear of the limousine. It propelled forward, extinguishing the high priestess' flame and forcing her to stumble backward. She tumbled to the ground and slid on the pavement on her ass before looking at me in complete shock.

My stomach heaved immediately as if my body were repelling the magic within me. I grabbed my chest and rocked in my seat as my insides began to shrivel.

Rene slid along the leather seat and wrapped his arm around my shoulders. "How did you retain your magic? What is happening to you?"

My body felt like my insides were turning in on itself. The twisting in my guts continued as I attempted to answer him. "I didn't possess that magic when I was alive. But whatever that was, it's... poisoning me." Maybe it could end here. Living a life in excruciating pain was not for me. My head turned toward the overseer as I gasped from the pain.

His eyes flickered with red, and I wondered if that was real anger. Was he about to kill me? A witch who turns was unheard of, but there was an argument that my magic had been so weak that I was practically a mundane. A witch who developed magic after becoming a vampire. That was a fricking unicorn. I simply shouldn't exist.

He seemed to look into my soul and look for something. I had no idea what it was, but I did know he was just as likely to toss me out of the limo as protect me. A crispy-fried vampire was not what it was cracked up to be, nor an experience I was looking to endure. Not when you were a newly turned vampire. Your skin had UV protection in the negatives.

Cassara leaned over and hit the button to roll up the window as Ursula pushed herself to her feet. "Driver, go now." She shouted as Ursula made it to the window and began to bang on it once more. The gravel crunched under the tires as we pulled out of the laneway and onto the street and she stared at me like I had two heads. But a Siamese twin was far more common than a vampire witch.

My body continued to shake, but the pain was easing, though my mouth felt like the tissues were turning to sand. My lip quivered as I tried to focus on healing the pain from within, without any idea if it was working.

Rene relaxed into the seat. "What is happening to her?"

Cassara shook her head. "I think her body is in shock, but that's a mundane reaction. It shouldn't happen to the vampire."

While the pain was receding, my body continued to cool. My entire body shivered as if I were lying on a bed of ice. "Make it stop," I whispered through blue lips.

Rene touched my shoulder. "She is unusually cold."

Cassara banged on the partition that separated us from the driver. "Go faster. Get us to the mansion."

Rene scooped me into his arms and held me against his body as every limb of my body shook. The warmth emanating from his chest was gradual but once I realized he could manufacture his own body heat, I leaned toward him and slipped my arms around his waist.

"What are you doing?" Cassara asked.

"I am simply warming my body."

"I didn't know you could do that?"

Rene glanced out the darkened windows. "An overseer has many useless powers."

Cassara was silent for a moment. "Since her shivering has stopped, I doubt she would agree with you."

I rested my cheek against Rene's chest until I began to feel as normal as possible for my new reality. "Thank you. I think I am alright now."

Rene hesitated before releasing me from his arms and positioning me on the seat beside him. "What caused your adverse reaction to using magic? I have never seen a vampire go into shock."

I grunted. "Until an hour ago, you'd never seen a witch turn. How am I supposed to know why using magic affects me so adversely? You think there's some kind of manual for this shit?"

Cassara grunted, but when I looked at her, the smile didn't reach her eyes. What did it take to scare a death dealer? Their leader. Me. A vampire witch with magic.

Rene's arm slipped around my shoulder, turning me toward him. "The coven is not forthcoming with their practices. There must be some spell or ritual that explains your transition and your magic."

My jaw dropped as I looked at him. "You honestly think I wouldn't have told you if the coven had done something to me? Are you that daft?"

Cassara covered her mouth and looked away, but this time the smile did reach her eyes.

"It's possible they did something after your death," he said.

"If the coven had a way to alter me so I would transition, it would've needed to have been performed when I was alive. Trust me when I tell you that no witch, especially Ursula, would condone this. We hate you. We train on how to survive a vampire attack. On how to dissuade humans from testing. I'm sure you know this." Rene nodded.

"We have had several meetings in the Twilight Conclave regarding the witches' interference in our testing procedures. Fortunately, many humans wish for immortality, especially when a married couple are both deemed worthy prospects."

"Then stop asking me stupid questions," I snapped.

Cassara had to turn in her seat and averted her eyes, but her shoulders shook, and it was obvious she was laughing. Since when did death dealers have a sense of humor? It went against everything I knew about the vampire kill squad.

Rene's eyes roamed over my face. "Do you have a death wish?" His voice still lacked emotion, and I wondered if I had gone too far. Cassara turned in her seat quickly and my doubts were confirmed by her wary eyes.

As much as I feared Rene, I would never pretend I was anyone other than me. "Pretty hard when I'm already dead."

"You are undead. There is a difference, and you have no idea what that means. Perhaps you would forgo the sarcasm and ignorance and learn about your species before you make any more undignified remarks."

Yeah, that uncaring response was straight out of the high priestess handbook. I had an entire childhood of rebuttals for being different. Not good enough. Weak. I would never beg to be a vampire or anybody's bitch. "Wow. You were the smart ass of the bunch, weren't you? What era were you spawned in?"

"I was turned over two thousand years ago," he said.

I expected him to be old but even I was surprised. Still, I would never admit that to him. "Well a lot has changed. Especially women."

His head tilted slightly. "Women were owned like cattle when I was alive."

I smacked his arm. "You pig!"

Cassara pursed her lips, but she grunted, and I could see her trying to stop from laughing.

I glanced at her. "What is so funny? You, of all people, shouldn't be okay with him degrading women."

She cleared her throat. "He's fucking with you, Raven."

I shook my head. "No way. He doesn't have a sense of humor."

Cassara leaned back in her seat, causing the leather to creak. "True. He no longer feels emotion like the rest of us, but he would never treat a woman with disrespect. Trust me, I know. I would've castrated him myself if he did."

I frowned. "But you have to obey him. He is your overseer."

Cassara glanced between me and Rene before she burst out laughing.

CHAPTER 10

Rene stared at his cackling death dealer. "Cassara, calm yourself. Your giggling is unbecoming of one of your stature and age."

Cassara grunted. "Whatever, your highness. How do you want things to roll when we arrive at the mansion?"

Rene glanced at me casually. "Raven is my responsibility. We need answers to how she came to be and an idea of what her evolution is. Her integration will be... challenging as it is."

Cassara leaned forward and opened the mini fridge between the seats. She grabbed a green wine bottle that was identical to the one I had smashed in the morgue. After flipping three crystal glasses onto their bottoms from the bar, she proceeded to fill them halfway. "That is an understatement, and you know it." She passed Rene a glass before offering one to me.

My fangs extended, and I accepted the glass but didn't put it to my lips. Cassara took a sip of her blood wine before I felt the trickle on my cheek.

Cassara froze as I stared at her. "Rene..."

Rene's hand snaked out and gently touched my chin before turning my face toward him.

I pulled back and wiped the blood-red tear from my eye. "I'm sorry. I didn't mean to get so emotional. Today has been a lot."

Cassara placed her glass on the bar. "It's not the fact that you are crying, Raven. It's the fact that you can."

"What?"

Cassara leaned on her knees, angling her body toward me. "Vampires don't possess human bodily functions. Blood hydrates us for lack of a better word. We don't excrete anything as our bodies absorb the nourishment we require."

I held up the glass in my hand. "Great. I am going to be the only vampire who has to get up in the middle of the night to go pee."

Cassara pursed her lips. "This could be part of your transition. It's a little different for everyone and a few vampires have retained a few human qualities during the first few weeks."

"So I just drive to the nearest bathroom. I'm sure you don't have them in your homes."

Cassara leaned back in her seat. "It's true the Shadow Bone mansion was built to our specifications, but we do have bathrooms. You forget that many of us have human families or lovers. We still bathe and shower, but many don't have toilets. I had one installed in my private suite, though."

"Really? Do you have a human family?"

Cassara smiled. "No, honey. I'm over four hundred years old. My human family is long gone, but I love human men. I'm trying to persuade Derek to be my next lover. I really hate it when a man plays hard to get."

I was so enthralled by Cassara and her story that I took a sip from my glass before I realized what I was doing. The sweet elixir tickled my throat, and I swallowed the taste of blueberry and mint. "You aren't what I expected, Cassara," I said honestly.

Cassara winked at me. "You might as well call me Cass. We will be spending a lot of time together over the next few years. You can ask me anything and know that as your mentor I will die before I allow any harm to come to you."

"I feel like I just entered witch school all over again," I said.

Rene glanced out the window as the trees flew by. The driver was going fast as Cass had asked, but the ride was so smooth, I had barely noticed. "There is nobody in any of my clans that can help you with your surfacing magic, so you must report any occurrences directly to me. You are my fledgling, since your attack was not sanctioned, and I was the first to… claim you."

I scrunched my nose at him. "Derek called you. It's the only reason you came."

"Yes, but that was unique. When a human is bitten, we investigate right away. Your body would've been remanded to the Shadow Bone Clan to see if you transitioned. As a witch, that didn't happen, but normally a foundling... a vampire who was killed by a rogue, is sheltered and mentored by the vampire who discovered them," Cass said.

"But since Rene has more important duties, he assigned you to mentor me and shelter me," I said.

Rene turned quickly. "Make no mistake, Raven. You are my fledgling. I have many duties, so Cassara will help me with your mentorship, but you will be housed with me."

Cass dropped her jaw but snapped it closed when Rene gave her a dark glance. It bordered on emotion but not quite. "What if she needs a toilet? Your suite doesn't have one. You don't even have a towel rack."

Rene smoothed his black tie. "Our suites have a connecting door. We will keep it unlocked going forward. If she requires a toilet, she can use yours and I will have anything she requires added to my suite."

"Like an extra coffin," I said before I realized I had said it out loud. "Sorry, Cass."

The death dealer's eyes remained on Rene. "No problem, honey. You are taking this pretty well, all things considered. Just keep an open mind, especially when it comes to his royal peskiness. I think we are in for a bumpy ride."

I took another sip of my wine. "I am sure. I wish I could explain what happened so I could put everyone's mind at ease, but even the smallest amount of magic should have made the transition toxic."

Rene's voice dropped, and I found myself turning and leaning toward him. "Do not concern yourself with things beyond your control. I will investigate the origins of your transition personally."

My lips parted at the hypnotic quality in his voice, before I forced myself to shake my head. "Stop it."

Rene arched an eyebrow. "Stop what?"

I pointed to him. "The thing you do."

He was silent for a moment. "What thing?"

"The resonance in your voice. Stop trying to hypnotize me."

Rene's lip twitched so slightly that I wasn't sure if I imagined it. "That is not possible with another vampire. Perhaps you simply find me attractive. It happens frequently with your kind."

Cass covered her lips with her hand but with her eyes cast down. I couldn't tell if she was laughing, or concerned.

"Don't flatter yourself. No witch would be caught dead with you," I snapped.

Cass cleared her throat. "And yet here you are, witch. Caught and dead." Her voice held a teasing quality that attempted to include me in her joke rather than make me feel like an outsider.

Shit! She wasn't wrong. Trust me to use the most inappropriate mundane saying at the worst possible time. I looked like a complete idiot and felt like one, too. "You know what I mean."

"Do I?" Rene asked with that same sense of dead superiority.

I stared out the window. "Any woman alive would be attracted to you. Right up until they discovered you have the personality of a lamppost."

Cass chuckled. "She makes a good point, Rene."

"Do not encourage her, Cassara."

Cass shrugged. "That is a mentor's job and I take mine very seriously."

Rene was quiet for some time. "For that, I am eternally grateful." There seemed to be more to the conversation. Maybe some kind of reference to their past or Cassara's origins. Either way, I was just too tired now to engage. The glass was empty, and it tipped against my leg as it drooped in my hand. He took it from me and placed it back on the bar.

The trees eventually filtered away and the large mansion with tall iron gates emerged from the countryside. The Shadow Bone Clan owned thousands of acres on the outskirts of Black Blossom County and the grounds were as pristine as the unusual home they resided in.

We turned off the road and onto the driveway that led to the mansion. The gate creaked open slowly, though it was unmanned. Not that any of the bloodsuckers could be out in broad daylight without some form of covering, but they likely had a security system to warn of outsiders' approach.

Even in the midday sun, the mansion appeared dark and foreboding with Gothic-style windows and black coverings. Many of which had steel bars covering them, adding to its looming presence.

The thick ornate door had a large, weathered door knocker, though I couldn't discern what the style was. And the spires atop it added to the ominous appearance.

There was a single fountain of a winged creature cast in stone with water pouring into the pool below, in the center of the turnabout in front of the massive building. I noticed one side of the building led to a secondary parking lot that was full of various black vehicles. All with tinted windows.

The driver stopped in front of the door and the breezeway that led to the vehicle. It was the only part of the structure that appeared to be an add-on. Rene took my hand when I moved.

"Allow Cassara to go first. We will go directly to my suite so you can change and acclimate to your surroundings. Few of the clan will be awake this time of day. These are our preferred sleeping hours."

Night owls didn't begin to describe vampire culture, but if my brief interaction with Rene and Cassara taught me anything, there was more I didn't know about their culture than I did.

"Okay," I said, pulling my hand from his.

Cass popped out of the limo as soon as Rene nodded to her and stood by the door before he exited. He held his hand out to me as I grabbed for the bag with my clothing. It had fallen on the floor when Ursula attacked.

"Leave them. I will have a new wardrobe provided for you shortly."

I snatched the bag and shot Rene a dirty look. Cass chuckled, but I allowed Rene to take the bag from me as I still had to hold the front of my sheet while pulling up my makeshift skirt.

He retained his grip on the bag when I exited the limo and intended to grab it from him. "Do you defy me out of principle?" he asked.

"Somebody has too," I said before I could censor my response.

Rene released his grip on my bag. "I see."

Cass opened the large front door as I attempted to keep my sheet in place and walk like I was wearing a couture gown. Isra could be wearing a burlap sack and make it look like he was walking on a runway. Me, not so much. I stumbled as I entered the main entrance.

The spacious foyer was dimly lit with heavy black drapes and gold brocade. The ornate wall sconces cast long shadows throughout the marble floors. The dark wood walls were lined with portraits of vampires from the past. Their clothing depicted the era in which they lived.

Two vampires stood with Dimitri at the base of the large staircase at the back of the foyer. Both men wore similar suits and red ties, denoting their stature within the Shadow Bone Clan. All of them looked at me with unveiled hatred and I couldn't say as I blamed them. If a vampire had walked into a coven retreat, they would be met with the same animosity.

I allowed Cassara to lead me and Rene toward the staircase, but Dimitri left his cohorts to intercept us.

"Rene, what are your intentions regarding the witch?"

Rene stepped between me and Dimitri. "She is my foundling and, therefore, my responsibility. Cassara will mentor her, as I must continue my duties to the clans. Tell me what information you have on her attacker."

Dimitri blinked. "I only returned five minutes ago. I haven't had a chance to..."

"If I wanted excuses, I would've asked the high priestess to run the investigation. If you are not capable of performing this task then I will assign another."

"No, Overseer. It is my highest honor to serve our clan. The rogue will be found and dealt with."

"Make sure he is apprehended and questioned. There was more to Raven's death than a simple attack."

"You do not intend to kill the rogue?" Dimitri asked with surprise.

"He will die by my hand. His connection to my foundling must be purged, but I require some information first. I suggest you find him soon, or my patience will wear thin."

Dimitri nodded and rushed toward a doorway. I blinked several times as my grasp on the front of my toga slipped. It was as if the fabric itself were made of lead and my eyelids were struggling as much as my fingers.

Cass stopped with her boot on the first step. "Rene, she is crashing."

I tried to focus on the strange things Dimitri and Rene had discussed. "What connection?" I asked before the room began to spin, and I slumped into Rene's arms.

CHAPTER 11

I didn't remember my bed being so comfortable. I rolled in the luxurious cotton and snuggled deeper into my pillow. But it wasn't the light smell of down or the memories of me waking in the dark that had my eyes fluttering open. It was the sensation of my nipples sliding against the soft fabric.

I patted my chest to confirm I was naked and remembered I had arrived in a morgue covering. My eyes went to the large bedroom with red and gold curtains and blackout blinds beneath them. I had noticed the windows were darkened on the outside of the Shadow Bone mansion and most had bars on the windows.

The large room had to be inside the mansion somewhere, but I didn't remember Rene and Cass taking me to a room. The foyer popped into my mind, and I remembered the room spinning. Had I fainted? Did vampires do that? Not that the current rules applied to me. I seemed intent on breaking them. No wonder Dimitri looked at me like he wanted to kill me.

There was a large walk-in closet that was cracked open, and I could see rows of suits inside. Men's suits. The kind

Rene wore. Oh shit. Was I in his personal bedroom? I prayed he hadn't removed the sheet and slipped me into his bed. Or worse, somebody else's.

The spacious room had a dark red couch and matching loveseat. While I couldn't make out the rest of the room, I was sure it was as lavish as the bedroom. How did I get myself into this?

"You look like a rabbit about to bolt," Rene said so softly I shivered.

I turned to the corner of the room. The wall scones flickered light over the center area, but he sat in the corner in a cream chair and seemed to blend into the shadows. Had he not spoken, I would have gotten out of bed and given him a peep show. Not that he would care. I pulled the sheet up to my neck and sat up. "How did I get here?"

Rene sat in his perfect suit with his legs crossed. He could be relaxing on a casual Sunday if you didn't know who and what he was. "You lost consciousness. It is typical in the newly turned. Fledglings require more rest than older vampires. Your body is still becoming accustomed to your new physiology."

I wasn't sure why it was comforting to hear I was doing something normal. Well, for a vampire, anyway. "I passed out. But how did I get here? Where is here exactly?"

Rene's fingers were curled over the thick arm of the chair and it made a slight cracking sound as he squeezed it. "You are in my private suite. In my bedroom, to be exact."

"Why did you remove the sheet I was wearing?"

"I assumed you would be more comfortable, so I had Cassara disrobe you and place you in bed." His voice retained that neutral and intoxicating resonance, but I detected something. Irritation maybe? I hadn't exactly been amicable to the vampire overseer.

"Okay. Can I have my clothes now?"

He motioned toward the closet. "I have a selection of clothing in the closet for you. Choose what you wish and if you don't find them adequate, simply order what you need. Cassara will have a credit card provided for you within a few days, but you may use mine until it arrives."

"No amount of money can make up for what I have lost," I whispered. Why was I being such a bitch? He was trying to be nice. In his way, but I kept busting his balls as if he were responsible for my attack.

"I am aware, Raven."

When he continued to stare at me, I gestured to the closet. "Do you want me to pull your bed apart? I am not parading in front of you naked. While I am sure your lovers have hit the thousands, I am not pulling a full Monty for you."

The chair squeaked as he glided from it. The grace with which he moved was criminal, and I kept my eyes on him as he approached the bed. "You make many presumptions for one so young."

"I'm forty..." As soon as I said it, I realized how stupid I sounded. While I was middle-aged in human years, I was a vampire toddler. How degrading was that? "Just go away."

He turned around so his broad shoulders were defined by his snug tailored suit. "Grab your clothes, Raven, before I tire of you issuing commands."

I scrambled from the bed and dashed to the closet, closing it behind me. My entire body felt like it was wound so tight it would snap at any moment. Did all new vampires feel like this or was that just being in Rene's presence? I focused on the array of clothing on the hangers before noticing the tags hanging from them. Every one was brand-new.

I pushed a hanger back so I could get a better look at one of the dresses. It was black velvet and from a well-known designer. As I flipped through the large selection, I found all the clothes were not only my size but high-end. I'd never been able to afford one of these outfits let alone all of them.

Still, I chose a soft black skirt and red blouse with a built-in bustier since I didn't have any undergarments. At least that's what I assumed until I saw the small dresser under the selection of shorts. The drawer was filled with lace panties of various colors and styles.

These all had the tags on them as well and I had to wonder if there was a shop in the mansion. They didn't have retail outlets at Shadow Bone, did they? Rene was right. I knew nothing about the vampires. Other than being undead and drinking blood, not much of my witch school teaching was true.

I slipped on a lacey boy short before pulling on my skirt and blouse. There were shoes beneath the clothes, and I chose a pair of knee-length black boots. The leather was like butter, and I loved the faux buttons up the back of them.

The full-length mirror was at the rear of the walk-in closet, and I barely recognized the woman staring back at me. My skin was paler, but only slightly, and it had a smoother quality. My size hadn't changed, and I was a little disappointed about that, but I was going to have to accept I would never be a size ten. Still, I looked amazing and couldn't wait to show Isra this outfit.

I exited the closet to find that Rene hadn't moved. He turned and his eyes roamed over me slowly.

"The clothes are adequate," he said. I wasn't sure if that was a compliment or him suggesting I could barely pull them off.

"That wardrobe cost more than all the furniture in my house."

"You live here now, Raven. Do you rent your current abode?"

"I own the house, but I have a mortgage. Jana lives with me, but it is still my home."

"The debt will be paid, and your daughter subsidized by the clan. It is our way, regardless of if you survive the transition."

"I already survived," I whispered.

"We don't consider a newly turned a success until the end of the second week. You will have cravings and must prove you won't act on them. If you cannot cull your instincts, then you will be purged."

I grunted. "Wow, you are mister warm and fuzzy, aren't you?"

"I have never been called such," he said with no sarcasm.

I rolled my eyes. "Shocker."

Rene motioned to me. "It is time to assess your blood. Vampires have certain... innate abilities. This is normally conducted as part of the testing process to determine a human's viability, but since your turn was unsanctioned, I will do it now."

I stepped back until I bumped into the closet door. "How do you test my blood?" There were no syringes in the room and no apparatus.

His fangs lengthened. "I will drink from you."

My chest squeezed despite the lack of air. "No way. I am not your personal juice box."

Rene held his hand out calmly. "That was not a request. All vampires must be tested and linked to me."

I held a finger up. "Listen here. You may be the overseer, but you are not sinking your fangs into me. No means no buddy."

He moved so fast I didn't detect the movement. One

moment I was looking at him and the next he was behind me, tilting my neck up. His fangs slid into my neck like a warm knife through butter and I winced from the short sting.

He took a long gulp as my eyes shut, and my body went into overdrive. His scent was an aphrodisiac, but it was nothing compared to the venom in his extra-long fangs. I would be all over him in seconds, and I couldn't let that happen. I could almost live with being undead, but turning into a vamp tramp in under two seconds was never going to happen.

The heat in my blood increased, and I realized it was now or never. I couldn't live with the consequences of falling under the spell of a man who felt nothing for me. How could this vile creature make me feel like this? Was it some form of torture? I felt like it. He was injecting me with his own version of vamp ecstasy, and he was potent.

I had heard about the effects of vamp venom. It was the reason young humans visited the blood clubs. It was its own kind of high, only it ended with shredded clothing and great sex. Or so I heard. Witches were forbidden to donate to the vamps whether it was a clinic or a blood club.

My body was vibrating as he took slow gulps from my neck. He seemed to take his time. Maybe he was analyzing my blood, as he said. Either way, I couldn't be this. I wouldn't be a thing he used at his disposal. Despite Cassara's assurances that he never used a woman. Maybe she had meant sex, not blood. It hadn't occurred to me at the time. He didn't need sex. He needed blood, and I had no intention of letting this continue. My brief existence as a vampire was about to end.

CHAPTER 12

As Rene's unique scent enveloped me and his lips moved against my neck, I recalled the class on vampire attacks when I was younger and learning to become a witch. It was back when they believed I had more potential.

My instructor had been an older witch who had lost several students over the years to rogue vamps. Blood madness was rare and even the coven leaders agreed that the vampires were ruthless when one of their members attacked a human, whether they were empowered or not, but the school taught us how to try to survive under overwhelming odds.

Vampires were far stronger, and an undead attacker afflicted with blood madness had no sense or reason. Our instructor compared it to a criminal on PCP. Reasoning went out the window, so you just had to relax and try to hold on until help arrived. Knowing what to do to survive hadn't helped me last time and this time, that training would ensure my destruction.

While his lips on my neck were soothing and warm, he didn't take large gulps or drain me quickly as the vampire at the shop had done. He seemed to savor my life-giving fluids and as my body continued to heat from the erotic sensations his venom caused, I tensed beneath his fangs.

All vampires had accelerated healing, but I was too young to have the benefits of those who had lived for hundreds of years. My fingers slipped around the door to the closet, and I used all my strength to push away from my attacker.

The older the vampire, the longer the fangs and Rene's effectively ripped the side of my throat out as I stumbled forward.

The feeling of ecstasy evaporated to be replaced by burning pain as Rene hissed. It was the first sign of real emotion and I found it ironic that it took my death to elicit a response. I fell forward as my blood pooled on the floor beside my neck and I gurgled, unable to create a single word. I was dying for the second time that day.

Rene bent over me and slipped his arms under my body before lifting me into the air. His fangs had retracted, and his tongue lapped over the wound at my neck. I had done my research when I was young. A fledgling couldn't repair the kind of damage I had incurred, yet as his lips moved over the serrated tissue, I could feel them melding together.

My eyes closed from the blood loss and the pain in my throat numbed to a steady tingle of electricity. It was strange and unlike anything I had studied about vampires.

I was floating on a cloud of heat and death when his voice whispered against my ear.

"What have you done Caramia?" His voice was so gentle it hurt my chest. Why should I care if my actions bothered him? He was a monster, and he just drank me like a tequila mix.

My eyes fluttered open, but I knew I wouldn't last long. His face looked ravaged, as if he had been put through a personal war. This face was nothing like the monster who had sat next to me in the limo. The one with eyes of obsidian. These eyes did not look dead. They looked betrayed. The weight of my eyelids proved too much, and they slipped closed.

I drifted in the same warm cotton softness I had woken to earlier, but as I opened my eyes, I turned to the chair where Rene had sat earlier. It was empty this time and my hand went to my neck.

I was naked again, and I swore under my breath. Cassara was going to need a talking to about personal boundaries. My hand moved over my throat to find it completely healed. I remembered Rene drinking from me and the damage caused when I pulled away from him. Did he have the power to heal his people? I was pretty sure I was dying when he ran his tongue over the wound. What was strange was his response. He shouldn't be surprised I didn't want to be a vampire, or that I wasn't interested in being his personal blood donor, but he had been angry and something else. He shouldn't feel anything. Cass had confirmed he was too old and had lost his zest for life.

I pulled my knees up in the bed. These sheets were even comfier than Isra's, and I slept over at his penthouse above the club often. Even in his bed. But we hadn't been more than friends since my pregnancy.

Lying around all day in Rene's bed wasn't going to solve the problem of my entitled overseer. He believed he had certain rights to the vampires who served him and that had to stop. He could kill me, but he wasn't going to make me his bitch. The sheet slipped down as I moved to the edge of the bed and was about to get up.

"What caused you to panic? I would never hurt anyone under my care," Rene said with that intoxicating and infuriating voice of his.

I froze as my eyes went to the closet. He was securing a new black tie and his hair looked slightly wet. His having to change because I ruined his last suit by bleeding out on it was probably minor, but I had to take the small victories where I could. There wouldn't be any big ones. I was a baby chick in the lion's den. I snatched up the sheet to cover my breasts as I looked away.

He seemed unaffected by my peep show, but he had likely seen thousands of women naked over the years and a forty-year-old with several extra pounds was probably a low notch on his bedpost. "Answer me, Raven."

"Does dictating to people ever get old?" I snapped.

"You are a guest in my house. I assumed you understood I was testing your blood, not draining you. My clan leaders report the schooling witches continue to receive. You are taught the procedure in the event of a vampire attack. You did the complete opposite."

"That was the point, princess."

"You wished me to kill you?" he asked.

"No. I wished you not to drink me like a big gulp, but you did anyway. Cassara said you didn't misuse women. No means no whether you wish to have sex with me or use me as a sippy cup."

Rene repositioned his tie and smoothed the front of his new dark gray suit. "Blood testing is mandatory and only required once. It is to confirm your blood is pure and that you are less likely to develop the madness that plagues our species. I will not drink from you again without your permission and I have not propositioned a woman in over fifteen hundred years for a physical relationship."

"Oh, I have no doubt of that. With your looks, money, and power, they probably line up to proposition you."

Rene remained quiet, and I knew I was right. Hell, if he

was a human or a male witch, I might have propositioned him myself.

I clutched the sheet to my chest. "Why am I naked again?"

"Your clothes were stained with blood. I had them removed. You can choose a new outfit from the closet. If you require modesty, I will turn around so you can retrieve them."

My eyes moved around the opulent room. "I can't live here with you. It's not right."

Rene glided to the chair that he'd sat in early and crossed his legs when he sat. "Do you have somewhere else you need to be?"

That was the question, wasn't it? I couldn't work or be around my family until I proved I was safe in the human community. Hell, I would never put my family or anybody at risk. But I did want to find out why I was killed. I had been targeted, and my being a witch had something to do with it.

"You wish to live, but you wish to do so by coven standards. That is not possible. We must come to an arrangement that is mutually beneficial."

I grunted. "I have nothing. What could I possibly offer you?" Yeah, my voice was bitter, but I spoke the truth. He had a gazillion dollars, and I wasn't even sure I still owned my home or shop.

Rene's eyes flickered with red. "And yet you are the first thing to intrigue me in over a thousand years. I actually felt irritation. I imagine that doesn't sound like much, but life lost its appeal to me a long time ago. It is the overseer's burden and curse to bear."

I had no idea what he was talking about. "You like me because I irritate you?"

His lip twitched. "Among other things. I do not process

emotions the way my brethren do, but your blood and your existence are a mystery to me. It is a challenge I welcome."

A mystery. "Great." I shouldn't be upset. My worthiness in my new clan boiled down to being something he couldn't categorize. Still, the reality that I had lost everything hurt. Not the store or the house, but that I would never go to the beach with my daughter. Never take another family vacation. My pain must have shown on my face as Rene moved like a jungle cat and sat on the edge of the bed.

The bed barely moved as he had little weight. His grace was matched only by his beauty, and I had to admire his athletic form, but I still couldn't figure out how he moved like he was walking on water. "You are sad. May I ask what vexes you?"

"Nothing much. Just the being dead part and not seeing my family."

"All vampires struggle with transition. Even those who petition for years to be turned. But you will see your daughter and friends soon. The human ones, anyway. You will simply need a chaperone."

I stared at his perfectly sculptured face. He didn't say it, but he inferred my witch friends would shun me. I thought about Deanna. We weren't just partners at Power Petals Florist. We had been friends since witch school. I had known her longer than Isra. Would she really shun me for an event beyond my control? I didn't think so. Deanna was a kind person and loved everybody. She had been the one to say she had no issue with vampire clients. The rest of the coven could bite me. I didn't expect any of them to side with me. Not now. "Deanna is my friend. We still own the store together and the rest don't bother me."

Rene's ability to remain as a stature was unnerving. When you didn't have to breathe, it gave new meaning to the word still. "Just don't be surprised if your coven is adversarial with you. Your priestess has complete control over your faction."

I cocked my head to the side. "And you have complete control over the vamps."

He nodded slightly. "I suppose I do. Except you, it seems."

I leaned forward before I forced myself to look away. Getting lost in Rene's stare was like falling down a rabbit hole. I wasn't sure there was any coming back if I allowed myself to be sucked in by his charm and sexiness. "Can I get dressed without you in the room, please?"

He stood. "Of course." He strode from the room with unearthly grace, and I couldn't stop myself from staring at him.

I was just pulling the covers off me when Cassara entered. "Hey! Rene said I could get dressed alone," I said, flipping the sheet back over my body.

Cass waved her hand negligently. "You asked him to leave. You didn't ask to be alone. If you aren't completely specific, he will turn it to his advantage. Besides, I'm your mentor and either Rene or I will be with you for the next few weeks. If it's any consolation, you don't have anything I'm interested in." She went to the darkened window and pulled the curtain back slightly so she could peek through.

I dashed to the closet. "I don't need a babysitter."

CHAPTER 13

It was difficult to pick a new outfit over the sound of Cassara's laughter. She was reported to be the deadliest death dealer ever. I could relate to her borderline rebellious nature with the overseer, but how had everybody missed her sense of humor? I didn't realize vampires retained those, yet many humans had told me that vampires weren't that bad. I assumed they meant that the undead in question didn't kill. Had witches been so wrapped up in their hatred that they never actually learned the truth about the other supernatural faction left in the world? Hatred and an unwillingness to see another's point of view had led to the war that annihilated the lycans. And the werewolves had been more like the witches than the vampires.

When the lycans were alive. Once bitten, they turned on a full moon, but learned to control the urge as they matured. They aged but at a far slower rate, but their instinct to fight within their own clans, for dominance and the right to mate, made it impossible to discern how long an alpha could live under the right conditions. The witches had many scrolls on the lycan culture, but only one report of a female who lived to be six hundred before she chose to join her mate in death after hundreds of years alone.

The witches studied lycan culture with our prejudice, and I often wondered if it was to see how Rene had won that war. While a lycan bite would turn a human, it was deadly to a vampire. Causing a slow, painful death as its insides liquefied. It all sounded pretty horrible.

"Are you sewing that outfit yourself, or do you need me to pick one for you?" Cass yelled from the bedroom.

I had let my mind wander and was still standing naked in the closet. I grabbed a matching lace bra and panties from the drawer beneath the clothes and slipped them on. The maroon lace was buttery soft. "Settle down, death dealer. Fledgling concierge wouldn't look good on your resume."

Cass chuckled. "That's true."

I grabbed a pair of black cotton capris and another pair of black leather boots. Then a red blouse that was the same color as my bra. Which worked out better once I realized the material had a sheer quality and you could make out the outline of my bra. The thin red leather jacket was the same color as my blouse, so I grabbed that too. I exited the closet and sat on the bed so I could pull on the boots. "Is it okay for me to ask about your transition?"

Cassara moved from the window to the chair Rene had sat in. Unlike the graceful overseer, she flopped down in an exaggerated manner. She motioned to my cell phone that sat on the dresser and I was stunned by her thoughtfulness. "Yes. It is always the first thing a fledgling asks. It is understandable to ask your elders about their human lives and their transitional journey, if you will."

"Rene turned you, didn't he?" I asked as I grabbed my cell and slipped it into the inside pocket of my posh jacket.

The smile fell from her face. "He has turned only a few

people himself in the last thousand years, but yes, I was one of them. I was dying when he found me, and it didn't take him long to figure out what had happened. He bit one of my attackers and learned the truth about my life and imminent death."

"You respect him. You would die for him, but you don't suck up to him like the others do," I said.

Cass winked. "Those that suck up to him, as you so eloquently put it, want something from him. Few people are comfortable in his presence for long. I don't want to be anything but what I am. A death dealer. If you break the rules you are going down. I am rarely commissioned to assassinate human or witch targets, but it has happened."

"That explains your rep. They didn't report your stunning good looks or snarky comebacks, though."

"I save the comments for those within my circle of trust. But if you have any sway with that sexy mortician, we should definitely add him to the list."

The death dealer with the hots for a human seemed so ridiculous, yet comforting at the same time. I wasn't exactly a woman who had made conventional choices, so her fascination with the humble human mortician was endearing. "I have met Derek a few times. He was there when my father died. He is kind and gentle. When I heard his wife left him, I was shocked."

Cass sat forward in her chair. "He was married?"

I nodded. "I only met her once when she ordered flowers from the store. Sharon worked for a law firm and a lawyer from the Seattle office came to town to input some new policies and recruit for their main office. She was only a secretary, but Sharon was beautiful, and the lawyer fell for her. He is a corporate lawyer with a mansion and several beach properties. Derek and I have some mutual friends, and

I was told he was devastated by her betrayal. It looks like Sharon cheated on him before she left him."

Cassara's eyes flickered with red. "That bitch. She lives in Seattle now?"

I dropped the boot I was holding to the floor. "Cass, you can't touch her. Human infidelity doesn't fall under a death dealer's purview. The human delegate would force Rene to stake you if you moved on a human."

Cass smiled, and it scared the hell out of me. "Oh, sweetie. There are so many things worse than death." She sat back in her chair, and I was pretty sure that the look she was giving me now was the one that had scared humans for hundreds of years. The sarcasm and laughter were gone, and she looked ready for the hunt.

"I'm sure I don't want to know what that means."

She shrugged. "I appreciate the information. Do you want to hear about my less-than-noble beginnings?"

I straightened on the bed. "Yes, very much. But will you tell me about Rene's origins first?"

"I would if I knew what they were. He predates all of us by over a thousand years, so that story will have to come from him, but don't be surprised if you never hear it. He is... fascinated by you. That may not sound like much, but for him to be intrigued by anything, even the mystery of your transition is huge for us. He has been losing interest for centuries."

"Is he going to kill me when the mystery is solved?" Cass grunted.

"No, and if he did, I would stake him myself. We don't turn on our own. You were blameless in this attack. You are a vampire and under his protection and mine. You are going to have a tough go since your origin story has spread through the clan like a disease, but nobody is stupid enough to cross Rene."

"Or you," I added.

She was quiet for a moment. "Nobody would go after me one on one. But many are unhappy with the power Rene has bestowed upon the death dealers. We are a newer addition to vampire culture."

"I didn't know that."

"You wouldn't. It happened over four hundred years ago and not even the vampires know the real reason Rene created us."

I placed the boots on the bed. "How did you meet Rene? You said you were dying."

Cass nodded. "I will start at the beginning, so you understand the nature of my attack. I was deemed worthless at the time."

"What do you mean?"

"My parents married me off to a local blacksmith in our village. I was his second wife, and he had one daughter, but he wanted a son. When I didn't produce any children after five years, he accused me of being barren and sent me back to my parents. I was simply a womb to him and while he didn't physically abuse me, I wanted no part of being his wife. Being labeled as barren stopped any potential suitors, so my sister's husband taught me to hunt game with him. My parents had passed and left the farm to her husband as women couldn't own land. We were cattle."

"That is awful."

"It was not a particularly good era to be a woman, that's for sure. Anyway, my sister was pregnant with her third child when Gustef attempted to have sex with me. I was handy with a knife and a better shot with a rifle than he was by then.

My sister Carol had been put on bedrest and Gus figured I should stand in for her and take care of his needs."

"What did you do?"

"I broke his nose and threatened to remove his balls the next time he touched me. In retrospect, if I knew what would happen, I would have slept with him. He didn't want me. He just wanted to get off and Carol was eight months into her pregnancy and bleeding."

I couldn't imagine a world where women had no rights. I knew about our past. But women were stronger magicians than their male counterparts, so we had magic to protect ourselves. A male witch would never beat his wife if he wanted to live through the ordeal. "He tried again?"

Cass grunted. "I wish. He went home and beat Carol. She lost the baby and went into a postpartum depression. It's had several names over the years. But the baby blues had been worse for her with each pregnancy. She blamed herself for being weak. When I finally told her the truth, she said she would rather kill him than have her boys turn out like him."

"You killed him?"

"I wanted to believe Carol's beating was a result of circumstance. Gustef's frustration with Carol's condition and his being saddled with me. An extra mouth to feed as he put it. I was happy to do chores, hunt, and help with the children. Samuel and Edwin were angels with a little hellion mixed in. They were too young to see the monster their father truly was and when he beat Carol for burning the stew because Sam had a fever, I knew he had to go."

"What did you do?"

"I planned his death away from Carol and the kids. I made it look like a hunting accident that occurred with his friends from the village. When Carol was informed her husband died, we pretended to mourn him, and Samuel inherited the farm with her as his caretaker until he was old enough to manage it himself."

"I can't say I blame either of you. Did one of his friends suspect you?"

"No. We got away with that one, but six months later, one of Carol's friends almost died. Her husband was far more abusive than Gustef, and Carol asked me to help her. That friend told another friend and within five years, I had dissolved several marriages in the most permanent way possible."

"I'm not sure which is worse. The fact that women had to be covert about contacting you for help or that your only option was to kill their husbands."

"It was a different time."

The silence was oppressive before I spoke. "How did you die?"

"There were rumors about the spinster of death. The men suspected I was behind the killings, but there was no proof, and I was careful to ensure the abusive men died in front of people they had trusted and that I had an alibi. In the end, it didn't matter what the authorities thought."

"What happened?"

"A fifteen-year-old girl approached me to help her. Her husband, Grant, was on his seventh wife and the previous six had all died under mysterious circumstances after they gave birth. All died before they reached the age of nineteen. The man was a horse trader and it turned out that livestock wasn't the only thing he procured for his clients. I investigated him and it didn't take more than two days before I planned his demise. Unfortunately, he began to beat his young wife while I was scouting his home and he stabbed her as I watched from outside. I knew he had men in the house. I should have walked away, and my stupidity cost me everything."

"You went in."

"Yes. I began beating the shit out of him, but his crew heard him cry out and five men burst into his office. His wife bled out on the floor, and he had his men hold me down as he beat me within an inch of my life. Then he stabbed me in the stomach and dropped me beside his dead wife."

My hand moved to cover my mouth. "That is awful."

"I wish that was the bad part. He left me there. Unable to move. I drifted in and out of consciousness, dying in agony like a trapped animal. I crawled to the door when I knew death was coming and my hand touched a clean leather boot. I noticed one of Grant's men dead on the ground outside, but I had already lost too much blood to survive."

"What happened next?" I whispered.

"Rene picked me up and cradled me in his arms. I will never forget his first few words. 'You have a choice, Cassara. I have need of a woman like you. The coming days will be difficult, but I promise you family and loyalty. You don't have much time and must choose.'"

"How did you know what he was?"

"His eyes flicked red. He showed me what he was, and I believed him. I chose to turn and when he offered his blood, I took it."

I wasn't sure how to ask the next question. I knew Rene had given her his blood. "When you bit him, did it affect you? When he bit me, my body was in full meltdown."

Cass nodded. "Oh yeah. I was all over him like a fly on shit. He is potent."

"You had sex with him, then." I didn't know why the thought bothered me. It shouldn't. They had been together over four hundred years ago, and I knew they weren't together now.

Cass laughed. "No, we didn't, but it wasn't for my lack of

trying. I was young and didn't know how to curb my urges yet. Rene would never have taken advantage of me like that."

I smiled at her. "I am glad, but I am sure you weren't the only one to try to get in the overseer's pants. The women must line up like fireflies in the night."

"They were called britches back then and Rene hasn't been with anyone since I have known him. When I grabbed his junk, he put me to sleep and explained my reaction was normal when I woke and apologized."

"How did your sister take the news of your death, or did you pretend to be human?"

Cassara's eye creased, and it was the first time she appeared to be in pain. "Grant was pissed that I had made him look weak. He knew I would have killed him if his men hadn't saved him. He retaliated by going to my sister's farm and killing her and the boys. Rene knew this before he turned me. He had killed Grant and his men before finding me. Their memories led him to me. He avenged my sister's death before he even met me. Then gave me a new family. I even have children in the vampire sense."

"Really?"

"Yes. Two of my death dealers were humans who were dying when I came across them. I have a few others as well."

"Huh, Mama Cass. Who would have thunk?"

Cassara dropped her jaw. "I can't believe you just said that."

I grabbed the boots from the bed. "Hello, vampire witch here. I think me and conventional went out the window a long time ago."

"It's about time," she whispered.

After zipping up both boots, I stood up. "That's why you are sure Rene will keep his word. He never let you down."

Cass nodded. "Not just me, many others over the years.

His loyalty is absolute. He will never turn on you unless you betray him. I don't recommend that."

"I know you would kill me," I said honestly.

Her eyes flashed. "No, Raven. What he could do to you is far worse."

CHAPTER 14

Cass stood up and motioned to the door. "On that note, I think you are ready for the tour."

I smoothed the front of my beautiful blouse. "This is going to suck, isn't it?"

Cass laughed. "We are vampires. There is always sucking involved, but I promise nobody will be rude if they want to avoid a spear in the stomach."

I smiled as I followed her to the door. "You can't kill your clan mates for being rude."

"Trust me, there is more than one vamp in here I would like to stake, but you have to hit them in the heart. Anywhere else and they heal after they call you every rude name in the book." She opened the door and exited the suite first.

I joined her in the hallway. "Why do I get the impression you are speaking from experience?"

She smiled. "Oh, the good old days. The clan is well aware of the lengths I will go to in order to ensure the clans adhere to the overseer's rules. I barely ever get to stab anyone anymore."

I laughed when she sighed in an exaggerated manner. My

gaze went to the various tapestries on the wall. They were one of the eras long gone and quite beautiful. The maroon carpet was plush and had an almost paisley pattern with inlays of black and gold. Even the crown moldings in the hallway were of the highest quality. As we neared the main landing that led to the three lower floors, I glanced around. "It looked big from outside, but this place is enormous." I placed my hand on the railing as we began our descent.

Cass motioned to the lower floors. "We have over two hundred vampires in this clan. Shadow Bone is one of the smaller ones. Ironically, it seems to cause the most trouble. I get posted here every hundred years or so."

I pulled my hand from the rail, and we stopped on the dais of the third floor. "You haven't always lived in the Shadow Bone Clan?"

She grunted. "Not at all. This is my least favorite location. I used to travel with Rene, but when things aren't being dealt with as Rene likes, he sends me ahead to assess a clan while he deals with another. I was originally a Shadow Blood, but I don't consider myself a member of any clan anymore. I am loyal to Rene, and so are the death dealers."

"So you are like Rene. An overseer to the death dealers."

Cass shrugged. "I guess you can look at it that way, but I don't have a single member of the death squad I don't trust. That is far from the case with clan heads."

We descended to the main floor, and several vampires were standing around chatting. Though it wasn't overly late in the evening, the grandfather clock chimed at eight o'clock as we stepped onto the tile of the main floor. The vampires were all dressed in couture clothing. All except me and Cassara.

A tall blond in a sleek black velvet dress and perfect

makeup approached us. "Cassara, is this your new witch?" she asked, before sipping the glass of wine in her hand.

Cass grunted. "She is Rene's newest fledgling. He has asked that I mentor her. I recommend you watch your tongue, Marissa. Rene has given me strict instructions to protect her. I wouldn't want to misinterpret your observations as a threat."

Marissa pulled her gloved hand with the jewel-inlaid glass closer to her. "I was not threatening her. I would never do such a thing to a fledgling."

"Then remember she is mine and Rene's. You know how protective I can be of my people. Your sire did not survive my response to his interference with my squad."

Marissa paled, which was quite a feat for a vampire. "I meant no disrespect, Cassara. Jean was an idiot to try to overthrow Rene. I was too young to understand the dynamics of the vampire clan back then."

"I am aware. It is the only reason Rene wouldn't let me kill you. That doesn't stop me from hoping he will change his mind though," Cass said sweetly before touching my shoulder and guiding me toward two men dressed in leather gear similar to Cassara's.

"You weren't exactly nice to her," I said with wonder. Why would she stand up for me when the blond was a full-fledged member? Clan life was proving to be far more complicated and not at all what I read about in witch school.

Cass grunted. "Why would I be? She is a clan cling-on. She will do anything to gain power. I have no respect for anybody like that. Man or woman."

The two men turned to her as we approached. "Cass." The one with dark hair and darker skin said. His features had a Mediterranean look, and he was good-looking, but his blond partner, while wearing a similar leather outfit with several weapons, could have been a model. His pale eyes fell on me, and he nodded slightly.

Cass motioned to me. "Val, this is Raven. Since her attack wasn't sanctioned and Rene was the first to claim her, she is officially his fledgling, but since he has many duties to the clans, I will be assisting him in her mentorship."

She had raised her voice, and I noticed several vampires glance my way. Most were surprised, but a few looked angry.

"Damn," the blond said when Dimitri exited an adjacent door and was walking toward us.

"Don't sweat it, Quinn. He is just here to try to intimidate Raven. Her status as Rene's fledgling is chafing his ass."

"Why?" I whispered.

Quinn stared at Dimitri. "Because Rene hasn't involved himself in the day-to-day duties of clan politics since Cassara transitioned. Him taking fledgling now is... surprising."

Dimitri stopped before the trio of death dealers and me. He nodded to them, but his eyes roamed over my body. "Raven, you are looking well." The words should have been a compliment, but there was a slight sneer in his voice. Still, he hadn't tried to kill me, so he had that over my high priestess. Apparently, they respected Rene enough to give him the benefit of the doubt. The high priestess was chosen because she was the strongest of the coven and I wondered if that was true of vamps. How did a new overseer ascend? I made a mental note to ask Cass once our unwanted guest left with his two sophisticates.

The two men standing behind Dimitri wore gray pristine suits similar in color to his and all wore red ties. They sneered at the death dealers, who remained stoic. There was definitely some clan tension here, and I was pretty sure it hadn't started with me.

"In the coven, the high priestess is chosen for her

strength. When the previous priestess dies, there is a ritual that tests the prospective witchs' magic. The strongest is elevated to high priestess. Is there something similar in vampire culture?"

Cass grunted. "Not exactly. We live a lot longer than witches. The last overseer before Rene died over two thousand years ago. He lost his mind as all overseers do... eventually and Rene was forced to..."

Dimitri stepped close to Cass. "How dare you? That is not a story for a fledgling. You are inferring our overseer is on the brink of madness. Your insubordination will not be tolerated."

Cass pointed to herself. "My insubordination? This clan is a shit show, and that has nothing to do with me. You are all wound so tight nobody brushes their hair without checking with you first. It's a farce and Rene is open about what happens to older vampires. He shows no signs of madness despite his lack of interest, which is more than I can say for you. If Rene wasn't protecting you, I would initiate the next election myself."

Dimitri's fangs lengthened. As his eyes flickered with red. "You will reap what you have sown death dealer. All your kind will. Sage will not be the only casualty this time."

Val grabbed Cassara's shoulder when she lunged toward Dimitri. "He's not worth it, Cass. Don't give him any more ammunition. Rene has enough on his plate right now with the Twilight Conclave tomorrow and Raven's transition."

I looped my arm around Cassara's. "Hey, you promised me a tour. Why don't we leave limp biscuit over here to his friends?"

Cass grunted as Dmitri turned to me. "You should choose your friends more wisely, Raven. Sage believed as you did, and as soon as Cassara and Rene ran off to another clan, she was mysteriously killed."

I glanced at Cass. Was the clan leader actually insinuating he had one of the death dealers killed? That was treason, wasn't it? "You killed her?" Cass tensed, as did the other two death dealers.

Dimitri smiled like a viper. "Of course not. She was a respected member of this clan, but her killer was never apprehended. We believe that somebody within the clan takes issue with the death dealers and Rene's lack of responsibility when it comes to policing them."

"So, they scare the shit out of you because you can't control them. You envy the fact that they are loyal to Rene."

Dimitri pushed past Val and stopped in front of me. "Do you wish to die?"

CHAPTER 15

If Dimitri wasn't dead, I was sure he would have had steam bursting from his ears. His eyes glowed like red LED lights in the darkly lit room. The wall sconce lights continued to flick splashes of orange color against the walls, but they were nothing compared to the crimson laser beams focused on me.

Cass inserted her body between me and Dimitri, and I was forced to step backward. "Back off Dimitri, she is under my protection."

Dimitri huffed. "Sage was as well and look how that turned out. You can't be everywhere, Cassara. Fledglings need all the allies they can get to succeed in a vampire clan."

The two vampire drones Dimitri had with him both sucked in a breath, and everybody turned when Rene descended the stairs. He looked like a forgotten god the way he moved. It was beyond graceful. He screamed that he was something other than human with each step, and the entire foyer went silent. That surprised me too. They had to be used to the overseer's presence by now, right?

He walked directly to us, and his perfect Italian shoes

didn't make so much as a scuffle sound as he walked on the tile. Heels were supposed to click when they contacted marble, but not Rene's. He stopped before us and turned toward Dimitri. "Dimitri, why are you threatening my fledgling?"

Dimitri's eyes returned to their dark chocolate color, and he smiled politely at his overseer. "There was no threat intended. She is yet to learn our customs and can't be held accountable for her ignorance. I was just about to ask her about her attacker so I could further my investigation into the rogue."

Rene's eyes remained cold. "I have identified her killer."

I sucked in a breath. "Really? Who is he? Do you know why he attacked me?"

Dimitri hissed at me. "You have no right to make demands on the overseer, despite his duty to mentor you."

Rene turned to me, and his tone softened. "I assure you, the hunt for Isaac is already underway. He is a member of the Shadow Demon Clan, and the clan leader has already been notified. It would be unwise for him to remain in Black Blossom County, but we will continue to search for him, as will the other clans. He has been excommunicated from the clans, but I want him apprehended. If anyone kills him, they will take his place for my interrogation."

Dimitri's jaw snapped shut. "The overseer does not cater to fledglings."

Rene stepped closer to Dimitri. "I will do and say as I wish. If you take issue, then challenge me for leadership. I am tired of your snide comments. The fight will hardly be worth the four seconds it would take me to kill you, but it may be more efficient to promote a new clan leader who can expedite my wishes without this... drama."

Dimitri lowered his gaze. "I apologize, Rene. I

overstepped. Your rule is absolute, and nobody wishes to challenge you. No vampire has your strength."

"Find Isaac. I want that traitor in custody before the Twilight Conclave. If you fail me, there will be consequences."

Dimitri nodded, but he glanced at me as he walked away, and there was nothing but hatred in his eyes. I was suddenly very thankful I had a death dealer bodyguard. She called it a mentor, but I had the feeling I needed Cassara's fighting skills more than her knowledge.

I waited for Dimitri to exit the foyer through the doorway he had entered before I turned to Rene. "How did you discover the identity of my attacker?"

Rene looked down at me. "I saw him in your mind. A death memory is very powerful. It was the other reason I needed to drink your blood. Isaac has made an unsanctioned kill. He must be taken off the streets for the safety of the community."

I crossed my arms. "You might have explained that part and I might not have fought you on the Raven juice box thing."

Cassara, Val, and Quinn all pursed their lips and glanced away as if one of the parties in the foyer was suddenly interesting.

Rene stared at me for some time. Everyone in the foyer did. Had I committed a crime? "Dimitri was correct in his assessment that you cannot be held accountable for your lack of knowledge of our ways. Your upbringing will make this more difficult than a human fledgling. I look forward to your education, Raven." He turned to Cass. "Walk with Raven and me for a few minutes. We will start her education together, but I must leave shortly."

Cass made a slight nod of her head to the two men and

they headed for the door. "No problem. Val and Quinn are going to look for Isaac."

Rene put his hand on the small of my back and led me toward the door Dimitri had exited from. The stares from the other vampires were one of shock, but I couldn't figure out what had them whispering to one another. Status appeared to be important in vampire culture and I had obviously overstepped mine by asking Rene for answers, but they hadn't seemed to question that.

Rene guided me to the connecting hallway, and Cass glanced at his hand on my back. It wasn't sexual. Isra often did the same thing when we went for dinner. He was the best date a woman could have, and I always looked forward to a night out.

While my best friend could rock a couture gown and five-inch platform heels, he was also devastatingly handsome in a tailored suit. Many women envied me when we went out and Isra didn't so much as glance at them. He didn't even check out the men unless I told him to. We had made a promise when I broke things off with him. Saying he needed to pursue his truth and if we were both single when we were seventy and sex was a distant memory, we would spend our last years traveling together and spoiling our grandchildren. I had effectively ruined that future and I rubbed my chest before Rene stopped me in the hall.

"Raven, what vexes you?"

I couldn't look at him right now. While Isra was gorgeous in a suit, Rene was godlike. I was never one to avoid my problems, but trauma piled up and I was starting to drown in the reality of my situation. "It's nothing."

Rene tipped my chin up, forcing me to look him in the eye. "I asked you what vexes you?"

"You may want to stop using words that have been out of

use for the last few hundred years. It makes you sound ancient."

"I am ancient," he said.

"Well, you don't look it. Could you pretend to have a cane or at least a few wrinkles? It's unnerving."

Cassara's shoulders quivered, and she pretended to inspect her silver staff.

Rene touched my cheek with one finger. "Your observation is interesting despite your sarcasm. A fledgling should not have the mental maturity to avoid my questions. You are immune to me."

"I think we both know what happens when you bite me, but you promised not to do it without permission."

Cass turned, and her eyebrows were arched. "Rene made a concession for you?"

"Raven, attempted suicide when I drew blood from her. She needs time to learn our ways and adjust to clan life. I do not drink my subjects, so it is hardly a concession."

Cass touched my arm. "Raven, don't ever do anything like that again. I swear I will kill myself and come after you if you do something so stupid."

My mouth opened and closed several times. She was sincere and looked slightly upset that I had reacted to Rene that way. "As long as nobody bites me, without permission, I won't."

Rene led me down the hallway. The decor was similar to the hallway upstairs, but this one had some ancient weapons on the walls. "You will have your debut in a few weeks. Once you learn the clan rules and have proven you can adhere to them… for the most part."

"What is a debut and what kind of rules?"

Rene paused outside two massive double doors. "I am sure you are aware we never kill. Those who choose to frequent blood clubs do so by choice. Both vampire and human. You will build an immunity to the smell of fresh blood, so you are unaffected if in its presence."

"A blood club. I actually have to feed on some random human? Gross."

Rene's lip twitched, and there was a flicker of red before it disappeared. Cass was watching Rene before he turned away from us. "Cassara, continue Raven's tour. I must attend to clan matters." He strode away as Cass watched him.

"Now, that was weird," she said.

I fiddled with my locket. "You just described my entire life... and death."

Cass placed her arm on the brass rail of one of the doors. "Maybe, but he looked upset... almost. I haven't seen flickers of emotion since I turned, and it was just the first few weeks. It was as if teaching me gave him a flare for life, if only for a little while. "

"Maybe he likes to teach. Honestly, I'm not sure how you can tell. "

Cass pushed open the large door and held it for me. "It's like the difference between a stone statue and a snail smiling at you."

I entered the ballroom and whistled. The polished wood floor was massive and conducive to dancing. Long crystal chandeliers hung from the ceiling and the brass accents complemented the gold crown moldings on the walls. There was a raised dais that acted as a stage or podium, depending on what event they were hosting, but every nuance screamed formality with an air of sophistication. There were black velvet booths lining the walls and dozens of circular tables with black tablecloths. My study of the ornate room was interrupted by a text, and I pulled my phone from my pocket. "It's from Cameron. He wants to know if I am okay. Will the PSO have been informed of my... situation?"

Cass nodded. "The human delegate was informed the moment you were attacked and after you survived. William was the PSO leader before being elected as the delegate. He will have informed his new team leader and their unit of your transition. It's protocol for new fledglings."

"Because we are high risk," I said.

"Yes, but they know you will have a mentor."

I read the next text when it chimed. "Am I confined to the mansion?"

Cass glanced around the ballroom. "Nope. As long as I am with you, we can go wherever you choose."

God, this was embarrassing. "I want to speak with him privately. At a restaurant maybe. Can you sit at another table for a little while? I know that isn't cool, but I just want a few moments alone and then we can visit Isra and Jana."

Cass held up her hand. "It's perfectly fine. Many attacks are not on unattached humans. There won't be any sex unless you want me to watch, but I can sit at a nearby table to give you privacy. I move fast. I just have to have eyes on you."

I tried not to pale at the thought of Cas watching me make out with someone, but she was trying to help. "Cameron and I were not at the physical stage yet. I just want to talk to him. He may not accept my new reality, but I owe it to him to speak with him personally."

Cass shrugged. "No problem. Just know that if you get hungry, we will have to excuse ourselves and feed you."

"You are bringing blood with you?" Cass tapped her neck.

"Always. Adult vampire blood sates a fledgling better than human blood. At least for the first hundred years or so."

"I am not drinking from you."

Cass sighed. "The venom doesn't work the same on the

same sex as long as you aren't gay. It's unlikely that you will grope me."

"Wow. That's so comforting... not."

"Listen, it is nothing personal, but you have to adapt. Fledglings are unused to the sudden onset of hunger. And they fight feedings. It's natural and a mature vamp is always a food source for you."

"I'm not feeding from you."

Cass stepped closer to me. "You will if you are about to put humans at risk. Not just mundanes but witches. Will you really endanger innocents like that?"

CHAPTER 16

I didn't want to answer Cassara's question. "That isn't fair."

Cass folded her arms. "Yes, it is. If I believed you wanted to hurt somebody, I would kill you myself. So would Rene, despite his... interest in you."

"I'm sorry. Public safety should be your number one priority and if I'm being objective, I would want somebody... babysitting a new vampire. I'm just a little old to be starting over."

Cass shrugged. "Not really. While older vampires were turned at a younger age as humans tended to procreate in their late teens a few hundred years ago, it is more common for people to request turning after they have children. Now the preferred age is thirty-five to forty."

"I have never seen an older vampire," I said.

"Yes, you have. Turning makes the skin more youthful looking, but it doesn't alter a person's features. We have had many turns of people in their early fifties. The testing process allows us to see if a person is viable, but it becomes less so after sixty or so."

"You prefer people who have had children. Human ones?"

"We do. When we have not diminished the human gene pool, but there are exceptions."

"Such as?"

"I was turned at a younger age because I was dying, but several of the young women were barren like me. They could not have children naturally, so that stipulation doesn't apply."

I glanced around the opulent ballroom before moving toward one of the black tablecloths. My fingers trailed over the soft fabric. There were no utensils on the table, only crystal goblets, but I noticed that several tables in the back had high-end china and gold cutlery. "Why do you have dinner plates?"

Cass joined me by the table and picked up one of the beautiful glasses. "Obviously, these are for blood, but the place settings are for the human guests. I assume you would want your family to attend your debut."

"They will be allowed here for this?"

"Of course. They are now an extended part of the clan. We will protect them and provide for them financially. It is our way when we accept a human into our clan."

I blinked several times. "It's amazing that you provide financial support." Cass couldn't understand what that meant to me. While Isra would always help Jana, she was only working part-time while she went to college.

"Yes. Since you are Rene's fledgling, she will receive a ridiculous amount. It's based on the net worth of the fledgling's sire."

"He isn't my sire."

Cass laughed. "He is now. You were attacked and Rene claimed you. Like me, you have unlimited funds." She unzipped her suit slightly and pulled a black card from the lining. "This is an unlimited card."

"What do you mean, unlimited?"

"It doesn't have a credit limit."

"That's impossible. Rene isn't the richest man in the world."

Cass laughed. "Wow, you are naïve."

"What do you mean?" I asked.

"He's been alive for over two thousand years. While he has each clan listed as owners of their prospective properties and holdings, he is the overseer. Technically, it all belongs to him. The reason the card has no limit is that there is literally nothing in the world he cannot purchase. Even I have no idea what his net worth is. Just trust me that if you can think of it, you can buy it." She glanced away with a grunt.

My eyes narrowed on her. "Why do I get the impression there's a story there?"

She placed the crystal glass back on the table. "There is. I was mad at Rene in the beginning. I was... am a bit animated, and it pissed me off that I couldn't get a response from him. If I was hurt, passed a test, or killed a vamp. His response was the same. He almost enjoyed teaching me things, but once I learned them, it was... nothing."

"What did you do?"

"I had tracked down and killed a rogue vamp who had gone on a spree and killed over twenty humans across Canada. It took me a week to find him and take him down. When I returned with him in chains, Rene just nodded and proceeded to inform me of my next task. I was under a hundred years old, and no other death dealer had been able to take that vamp down. He had killed two of us the day before his capture."

"I can understand you being pissed."

"No, you don't. I knew why Rene was like he was by then. My reaction was unwarranted."

"I'm guessing you went on a shopping spree?"

"I bought a mansion in Quebec City and a hundred acres surrounding it. Then I furnished it and told Rene it was a birthday present. He inspected the home and didn't even look at the ridiculous amounts of money I had spent. He said it would make an excellent clan home."

"What?"

"Yeah. He made me start another clan, and Shadow Thorn is now our youngest and located in that very mansion."

"Who named it?"

"I did. Because Rene is a Thorn in my side sometimes. Too bad he can't appreciate the irony."

I chuckled. "I think he got the last laugh on that."

"Oh, yeah. It took me fifty years to get that clan up and running smoothly and I still had to travel with Rene and communications were no picnic back then. It was a nightmare."

"You have lived an eventful life."

"As will you. Now, do you want to go on that date?"

"I do and I want to see Jana," I said.

Cass touched my arm lightly. "Then let's go. Do you want to change first? You look gorgeous."

I followed her through the large door to the hallway. "Can we pop by my home first? I don't think Jana will be there. She is likely with Isra while she processes what happened to me. She has a room at her father's home, too."

"Sure. We will take the truck and you can retrieve any personal items you wish to bring to your new room."

"Thank you, Cass. I appreciate everything you are doing for me. I'm sorry if I make things difficult for you." I never thought I would see the day I apologized to a vamp. While I didn't want much to do with the clan, I found I liked Cass. Maybe I could stay in her room. Rene scared the crap out of me, and it was more about how my hormones reacted to him than the length of his fangs. My mind fantasized about what else was long, but I nipped that train of thought quickly.

We exited the mansion, and I had to admire the floodlights that illuminated the Gothic exterior and the fountain in the center of the roundabout. The vampires had unlimited funds, and it showed. Despite what Cass had said, I didn't want to live off of Rene's money.

"Am I allowed to have a job?" I asked as I got into the passenger's side of a black Escalade.

Cass jumped into the driver's side and inserted the key before the engine roared. "Of course. Do you think being a death dealer is a pansy-ass picnic?"

I stuttered before my words exploded in a rush. "No, it... No. I thought maybe..."

Cass laughed as she pulled out of the side parking lot. "I'm just fucking with you. Everyone works for the clan in some capacity. Once you have acclimated to our lifestyle, you can see what vocation best suits you."

"Oh... what if I want to continue to work at my store?"

Cass was quiet for a moment. "Some vampires had human jobs we integrated into our lifestyle. Rene doesn't have a flower shop. We will have to wait and see. You may find your interests have changed in a few years."

"Years?"

"Yes. You can't work alone in the human public until you are fully vetted. You will earn your privileges to be unchaperoned."

The streetlights flashed above me as I stared at the houses rolling by. We were still in the rich area of town where the mansions spanned several blocks, though none were as large as Shadow Bone. "Okay."

We drove in silence as the cultured lawns turned to smaller parcels of land and expensive but moderate homes. The turnoff onto Lily Street was familiar. While we were over twenty city blocks from the start of the Shadow Bone property, I was the closest empowered human to the property. It wasn't a hard rule as many witches had human families, but the closer a witch was to the vampire clan, the less valuable they were to a coven. I had never had much worth in Ursula's eyes, so when I bought a home in the middle of mundane-owned properties, nobody was surprised.

I was about to tell Cass which home was mine, but she pointed to the GPS. "747, right?"

"It sounds big but it's only a two-bedroom. You will feel like you are in a shoe box when you get inside."

Cass laughed. "Hasn't anybody ever told you that size doesn't matter?"

I smiled as I exited the SUV. "Only a guy when he was talking about his penis."

Cassara's shoulders quivered. "Yeah, I bet." Her eyes moved over the exterior of my home. The white house was illuminated by three patio lights on the deck, but the lavender trim appeared darker in the moonlight. "It's cute. I like the tulips and roses." She didn't strike me as a flower lover, but I was proud of the array of colorful blooms on the exterior of my home. I had the smallest house on the street, but also the most beautiful garden. I smiled as I ascended the steps.

The doormat was crooked, and I bent down to straighten it before unlocking the door. Jana knew better than to leave it open and I entered the small living room and motioned Cass to enter. The death dealer looked a little out of place in the slick one-piece leather outfit and clipped weapons as her eyes roamed over the matching cream sofa and loveseat with lavender cushions. The oak coffee table and side tables were newer, as was the candy bowl between two small plants atop it.

I motioned to the hallway. "Can I just grab a few things from my room? You can come with me if you like. Jana isn't here or her purse would be by the door."

Cass stared at the TV on the wall. "Take your time. I can wait out here. Where is the remote?"

I pulled the top of the ottoman off to expose the storage space beneath it with the remote, a book, and a stash of chocolate bars. "Here."

Cass sat on the couch and grabbed the remote before I replaced the lid and headed for my room.

The pictures in the hallway were from the last twenty years. Most were of Jana in her school years, but a few were of me and Isra. Each photo reminded me of the future I would be denied and the past I would be forced to confront. I closed my bedroom door and went to my dresser.

The small box of jewelry wasn't worth much, but several items had sentimental value. As I picked through the gold necklaces and my grad ring, I realized that the only piece I needed was the one I wore. My locket held pictures of the two people I loved. Everything else could go to Jana. I moved to the closet and grabbed the pink suitcase on the floor.

I used the case for our trips to the beach and now I would take the few items that were dear to me. They seemed pretty lame compared to the closet I now had at the Shadow Bone mansion, but none of those new outfits screamed comfy night with a chick flick, so I grabbed my yoga pants and flannel nightie before loading a few other things into the case.

There was one pair of heels I never wore as they were too fancy, but Isra had purchased them for me and if I had to do that debut ball thing, I was wearing them. Only I would know they came from drag queen couture. After going through my drawers and grabbing a few more items, I sat on my bed. When most of the life you could take with you was in one pink suitcase, it gave you a unique perspective on life. Mostly that mine was over.

My daughter needed me to be strong, and while she would know I was a vamp by now, she would be in as much shock about this situation as I was. There was no manual for a witch's turn, and I began to fear what repercussions could come down on my daughter as a result. Cass had promised to protect her, and I had the feeling that the death dealer didn't lie. She didn't need to. If you stepped out of line, she killed you.

I exited my room with the pink case in my hand. "I will just take this for now."

Cass clicked off the news and stood up. "Excellent. Where are you meeting, Cameron?"

"Sorry, I forgot to tell you. I'm meeting him at the Autumn Knight. It's a steak and seafood restaurant. It's one of my favorites, but we are sitting in the lounge. He said he would eat ahead of time."

"That is thoughtful of him. Let's go."

I exited the house and locked the door behind me. There was a rock in my chest as if I would never see my home again, but that didn't make sense. Jana would live here, and I would visit in the evening hours. I placed the suitcase in the back seat and waited while Cass started the vehicle. My heart squeezed as we pulled out of the driveway and my phone beeped.

I pulled out my phone. "Cameron is in the lounge."

CHAPTER 17

I stared at the exterior of the restaurant as Cass turned off the engine. "Cameron is sitting on the second couch. Do you want to take a table close to us? The other couches appear to be full."

"No. I have a decent view from here. You go ahead. This isn't really my style."

I nodded and exited the SUV before heading through the large oak door with a brass handle at the front. The petite blond girl standing behind the small podium with a map of the lounge and restaurant smiled at me as I entered.

"Are you looking for seating in the restaurant?"

"No. I am meeting a friend in the lounge. He is on one of the couches." She motioned to the left, which led to the dimly lit lounge. "Please go ahead."

The lounge was almost as stylish and sophisticated as the restaurant, but boasted a more comfortable atmosphere. Since the two were connected, it offered a smaller menu and focused on appetizers and drinks.

This time of night was busy for any well-known establishment, and a few tables or couches were empty.

Cameron waved to me when he saw me enter, and I smiled as I approached.

"Hey," I said as I sat on the couch beside him.

"Hi, yourself." He smiled, but there was a wariness to him that hadn't existed on our previous dates. Not that I could blame him. He was well-versed in the volatility of fledgling vampires and glanced around. No doubt looking for my chaperone. Still, his sandy-brown military-cut hair was freshly shaved, accenting the strips of gray and his tight black T-shirt accented his athletic body. I'd always appreciated his sense of humor and his no-nonsense take on life.

"Do you want a drink?" he asked, and while I knew it was a habit, I flinched. "Sorry, I didn't mean..."

"It's okay. I am going to have to get used to it. I'm too new at this to know what to say or how to react yet. Cass is in the SUV, so you are safe."

He grunted. "I'm a PSO-trained operative. I have taken down a vamp or two, but I know you. This will just take some getting used to."

"You would actually consider continuing our relationship. I know your views on vampires. Hell, I shared them until I woke up as one. In truth, I'm finding that my coven training wasn't completely accurate."

Cameron took a sip of his beer. "Really? How so?"

"Just the clan dynamic. I haven't started training yet, but Cassara isn't what I expected. She is funny and... kind."

Cameron blinked before putting his drink back on the coffee table. "Cassara James. The death dealer. She is your chaperone?"

"Yes. She is also one of my mentors."

"Wow. That's surprising. I thought the lower class... level vamps recruited and did training."

"I wasn't recruited. Rene was the first to discover me, so he is responsible for me."

Cameron froze. "The overseer is your mentor?"

"Yeah, he assigned me Cass, as he has so many other duties. I doubt he is happy about it, though he isn't happy about anything."

Cameron looked like he wanted to be sick. "Okay."

"I'm sorry. I know you were worried about me, and I am bitching at you like this has anything to do with you."

Cameron took my hand, and it felt warm. I assumed mine felt cold to his as I couldn't warm my body like Rene could. "It's okay. This is uncharted territory. Even the PSO is unsure how this happened. You will be the topic of conversation at the Twilight Conclave."

"Great," I said sarcastically.

He winked at me. "You look beautiful, by the way."

I glanced down at my designer outfit. "Vampire genes, I guess."

"You were beautiful before," he said.

I stared at him for some time. "Are you sure you're okay with this? I completely understand if you're not. It will be some time before I'm allowed in public without Cass watching me." I didn't mean to insinuate that there would be no sex when it was obvious on our last date we were headed in that direction. The kiss he had given me at my front door may have gone farther, if my daughter hadn't been home that night.

"Absolutely. I'm a mundane. We have relations with vampires all the time. My animosity toward vampires is more because the ones I meet are usually breaking the law." He was right. If he was dealing with a vamp on the job, it was prior to Cass being aware and usually when a human was under attack. He had every right to hate dealing with rogue vampires. They killed a lot of PSO operatives over the years.

"Thank you for not holding this against me. I know most of my coven will."

He grabbed his beer and took another drink. "You mind telling me about the attack? The overseer hasn't shared the name with the PSO yet."

"I had never met him before, but he told me I was targeted. He wanted to kill me specifically, so there is more to this than just a witch kill."

His eyes narrowed. "Are you sure?"

"Yes. He said I was chosen because I was a low-level witch and didn't contribute to my community. He planned to kill Jana, but she escaped. He promised not to go after her now, but I don't trust him."

"I guess not. I will make sure the PSO is aware your human daughter was targeted. That is unacceptable." I was sure he didn't mean to say a witch being targeted was, but my shoulders sagged just a bit before I recovered.

"Thanks."

He leaned back in his seat. "So, how do you plan to manage a mundane daughter and a drag queen best friend with vampire life?"

"Both Jana and Isra will accept me. They don't have issues with the vamps. They get vampires at the club sometimes. They love me, but the coven is another story. They want me dead."

Cameron shrugged. "They can't touch you without starting a war. There is no doubt you are a vampire and that would break the accords."

I clasped my fingers in my lap. "I know. They think I'm still a witch. It's complicated."

He rubbed his hand on his jeans. "That's for sure. Tell me

what you are allowed to do in the next few weeks. Is a movie off the table?"

I smiled. He knew I loved going to dinner and a movie. The first was now off the table, but the cinema was a nighttime activity I could still enjoy. "Yes, I can definitely..." I paused when the entire room went quiet. It wasn't just the lounge, either. The hairs on the back of my neck prickled, and I knew who had entered the lounge reception before I turned.

Cass was beside Rene and while he held the same look of disinterest he always did, she looked furious. Her eyes flicked with red pinpricks as she followed her graceful leader to our table.

My jaw dropped when Rene sat in the chair opposite us, and Cass took up a position behind him with her hand on her silver staff. "What is going on?"

Cass forced herself to smile, but it was like her mouth was full of razor blades. "I apologize, Raven. Rene has altered some of the protocols for fledgling vamps and wishes us to return to the mansion. We can visit your daughter soon, but we need to go over the new rules."

I glanced at Cameron, but unlike most people in Rene's presence, he didn't look scared. He looked like he wanted to murder the vampire overseer. "What new rules?"

Cameron put his hand over mine but kept his gaze on Rene. "He isn't allowed to keep you from your family. I am well-versed in transitional protocols. He can't change the rules human by human. You don't need to go anywhere."

This was not how I expected to spend my evening. Every set of eyes in the lounge was on me and several couples from the restaurant stood by the entrance to watch the byplay between my date and the overseer. I glanced at Cass. "I don't know what to do."

Cass shot Rene a dirty look, but he was in front of her,

and he didn't see it. Whatever Rene was doing was not to her liking, and I feared for anyone who got in her way. "It would be easier if we took this discussion home. I have a few words I wish to share with our illustrious leader." There was no doubt those words were not warm and fuzzy.

Rene nodded. "I wish to hear my death dealer's observations, but I must take Raven home. She is *mine*, and we have much to discuss."

I knew he meant I was this fledgling, but Cameron looked unsure after his declaration. "I am sure Cameron and I can reschedule so…"

Rene stood. "That would be inadvisable."

Cameron stood up to Rene. Though he was tall, he lacked the height of the overseer. "While I am aware of transitional protocols, you vamps are secretive about new turns and internal politics. The supernatural war left few documents about life before, but the vamps, Lycans, and witches never got along with anyone except the mundanes. You all need us, but none of us needs you."

Rene cocked his head to the side. "I must remand Raven to the mansion at this time. Please stand aside or your human delegate will be notified. I have complete control over fledglings prior to their clan ascension."

Cameron huffed. "I can have my team here in five minutes."

Rene nodded. "And I can be home in seconds. Do you really wish to start a war over a fledgling?"

"She isn't just any fledgling," Cameron snapped.

Rene glanced at me. "That is true. She is not."

I got up and moved to Rene's side. "It's okay Cameron. I need to find out what this is about."

Cameron moved away from us, but he grabbed his phone and began talking to someone as Rene turned to Cass.

"You allowed her to come here."

Cass nodded. "Yes. She was inside the entire time and never showed any sign of... Weakness."

"That is not the only reason you were assigned to her," Rene said. There was a hint of a reprimand, but I couldn't tell what he was attempting to imply.

Cassara looked as if she'd been slapped and glanced away. "I understand." I liked my vampire instructor and if I had done anything to get her in trouble, it wasn't intentional.

I grabbed Rene's arm. "Stop it. If I did something wrong, it's on me. Don't take it out on Cassara. You said I had time to learn the rules and Cass thought I was allowed to come here." It had to be the location because other fledglings met with human lovers and family.

Rene's eyes moved to my lips. "Will you return to the mansion?"

I moved closer to Cameron, and he put his hand over the speaker of the phone. "Hey, I am going to head home with Cass. I will text you once I get this sorted out."

Cameron looked like he wanted to argue, but he nodded and returned to his conversation as I went to Cass. "Let's go."

CHAPTER 18

Rene was like a walking perfect statue as he led me from the lounge of the Autumn Knight restaurant. Every person in the building had stopped what they were doing to stare at Rene. He was rarely in public, and everyone was curious about him. Considering his ridiculous good looks and unearthly grace, I couldn't blame them. It was like watching a refined panther stroll through a public domain. If said predator could pull off a five-thousand-dollar suit.

I kept my head down to avoid the dozens of eyes on me. The tingling between my shoulder blades alerted me to Cameron's anger as I left. He had every right to be angry and I would try to make it up to him once I had proven I wasn't going to snack on him or the other patrons. My pace quickened as soon as we exited, and I was about to rush to Cassara's SUV when Rene grabbed my arm.

His touch was light, but his hold was unbreakable as I attempted to pull from his grasp. "Let me go."

Rene did as I asked but motioned to the limo. "You and Cassara will ride with me. I have arranged for her vehicle to be retrieved by another driver."

Cassara's eyes narrowed on Rene. "What is going on? You are acting like a jealous teenager, but we both know that isn't possible. You weren't this insufferable with me." Her voice was waspish, but it also held a trace of something else. Fear. Concern. I wasn't sure, but I figured it took a lot to rattle the death dealer.

Rene opened the door to the back of the limo and motioned for us to get inside. "We will address your concerns on the ride home."

Cass motioned with her head for me to follow her, and I ducked down to enter the limo. It was the same one we had ridden in earlier. Only the glasses had been washed and put away. That or he had a fleet of limos that looked the same. I wasn't about to check license plates and I seated myself against the far door opposite Cass before Rene sat beside me.

He didn't even try to put distance between us as his arm slipped over the back of my seat and rested above my shoulders. He crossed his legs, but they rested against mine.

I pushed his body slightly. "Do you have to sit so close? The limo is massive." He didn't answer me as he turned to stare at Cass.

Cassara looked paler than usual and stared at me with fear in her eyes. "What are you doing, Rene?"

"I can't tell how this ends, Cassara. You know the likelihood of progression being... a positive one is extremely low. I have prepared you for that eventuality."

Cass flinched, and her fear was replaced by pain. "Is there a chance..."

"There is always a chance. But that choice is not up to me. You know this."

Cass nodded. "Why now?" she whispered.

Rene's hand dropped from the back of my seat and lifted

a strand of my black hair. "Some things remain a mystery, even to me. Honestly, I did not believe this was possible."

I raised both hands in the air. "Hello. Fledgling here. I have no idea what you are talking about."

Rene wound the strand of hair on his finger as if it were a snake. "I know. I will explain in time. You need to learn about clan life and your role within it before you are burdened with... other things."

Cass slumped in her seat and placed her elbow on the interior door handle so she could stare outside. Whatever Rene had said had bothered her, but she seemed lost in thought. "She is strong." She whispered so low I wasn't sure I heard her properly.

I hated this cryptic shit, and I grabbed the lapel of Rene's suit. "Listen. You may be the overlord or some shit, but if you lie to me or gaslight me, it will not end well for you."

"I am an overseer, not an overlord, but you are deliberately trying to provoke me. Why?" he asked in that infuriatingly monotone voice.

How did anyone deal with a man like Rene? I released his lapel and shoved his leg, which was as immobile as his body. His response was to slip his arm around my back and pull me closer to him. It was almost like a cuddle. Well, if a statue could do such a thing. His body was like granite. "Cass, help me here. Is he always so handsy with his fledglings?"

Cass glanced at me. "Not with me. Whatever this is, it's new."

I glanced up at Rene, but as my eyes moved over his neck, they fixated on the sweet smell of his blood. Why could I smell it? I hadn't noticed it earlier, and a sizzle of electricity arced through my intestines. I remembered the feeling from my transition and glanced down quickly, clasping my hands together.

"You are frightened, Raven. Why do I scare you so?" Rene asked casually.

It was understandable he could sense or smell my fear, but it wasn't of him. It was that my fangs had extended in my mouth, and I very much wanted to bite him. As if the hunger pains weren't embarrassing enough, my core clenched with the other desires associated with biting Rene.

"This is a lot. I just want to be alone for a while."

"That is the one thing we can't allow. Humans are allowed at the mansion at times, and mature vampires are a food source for you. Attacking a clan member is a death sentence for a fledgling. Cassara must remain with you at all times when I cannot."

There were so many things I wanted to say. "You are really annoying." Yeah, it was lame, but I had to focus on the pain slicing through my guts and keep my voice even. I flinched when the limousine came to a stop in front of the canopy that led to the front door. It wasn't needed at night, but it had fairy lights scattered over it that I hadn't noticed during the day. The effect gave the mansion an ethereal quality.

Cass coughed into her hand. "You have no idea."

"Cassara," Rene chided, though there was a hint of affection I hadn't noticed before.

The death dealer's head snapped up, and I suspected that was new for her, too. She stared at Rene for some time before turning to me. I flinched slightly as Rene opened the door and exited the vehicle. He held his hand out to me, and I blew out a breath as I accepted his help. There was a good chance I would end up on the ground if I didn't.

Rene slipped his hand around me and placed it on the small of my back as Cassara exited the limo and followed us. The pain increased with every step, and I groaned when a young vampire opened the front door to allow us access. While the foyer had been occupied by a few clan members when I left, it was now a beehive of activity. Murmurs and whispers echoed around us but fell to a hush when Rene stopped to wait for Cassara.

My death-dealing mentor moved to Rene's side. "She needs to feed now."

Rene glanced down at me, and his lip twitched. "Next time, do not wait until you are in pain. I am not as adept at social cues as Cassara."

If that was some kind of apology for not realizing I was in pain, it was a pretty bad one. How did you live over two thousand years without understanding humanity? He was born human, right? The thought of drinking blood still made me queasy, but it was preferable to the laser beam eviscerating my intestines. My response died on my lips as Dimitri pushed his way through the throng of vampires.

"Rene, what is the meaning of this?"

The overseer's hand moved slightly on my back. A twitch. Irritation maybe? "To what do you refer, Dimitri?"

"We received a call from the PSO. Raven's boyfriend said you interfered with their date. He was seeing her prior to her death and has the right to be in her presence."

Cass pointed at me. "Look at her Dimitri. She needs to feed. Public safety comes before any other rules. She chose to leave. Rene didn't force her."

Dimitri's gaze moved over me as I winced. "We should continue this debate in the feeding room."

Rene nodded. "I concur." He led me to the hallway that led to the ballroom, but we passed it and went to a small door at the end. He opened it and we found four tables with glasses and a medical station, which surprised me. Vamps didn't require any medical attention, did they?

Cass grabbed a black bottle from one of the tall wine coolers and poured a glass for me. When she held it out to me, I turned away.

Dimitri snorted. "She may have turned into a vampire, but she grew up as a witch. Her hatred of our kind cannot be erased with a simple glass and some kind words. She will not make a worthy addition to this clan."

Rene stepped up to Dimitri. "Since when do you decide what is best for the clan's future? Were you promoted while I was attending to my fledgling?"

Dimitri paled as his hand reached up and smoothed his red tie. "Of course not. You have always allowed me to vet potential clan candidates. I assumed..."

"Do not assume anything. Raven is the only witch to survive a vampire attack. She is unique, but more importantly, she is *my* personal fledgling. You do not have any authority over her welfare. I take my duties very seriously Dimitri, and I have not accepted a fledgling since Cassara. Be very careful where Raven is concerned. My death dealer has a spear with your name on it, and I have discouraged her from using it on you."

Cassara's lip twitched, and I had the feeling that she was looking forward to Rene loosening her restrictions. There was definitely some bad blood between Dimitri and Cass and when I wasn't having my insides microwaved, I would ask her about it. She grabbed a syringe from the medical station and stuck it in her arm. Once she had pulled enough to fill the vial, she moved to my side. "This will take the edge off." She injected her blood into my vein, and the laser in my stomach subsided.

"Thank you. Can I feed like that all the time?"

Cass shook her head. "Just in the first few weeks. You still have a human bloodstream and your own blood to supplement this. Once the transition is complete, you will need to drink, whether it's from the vein or a glass."

Dimitri shook his head. "Pathetic."

I wrapped my arms around my middle. I hadn't been there a day, and I was disrupting the clan. The weird thing was, I cared. I didn't want to make things harder for Cass. In a lot of ways, she seemed to be as much an outsider in the clan as I was. Even Rene seemed... apart. Like he didn't belong. Did having that kind of power and money alienate you from those around you? If that was the case, I couldn't understand why anybody would seek it.

Dimitri stared at me for some time before turning to Rene. "The human delegate called to inform us the high priestess has requested we convene the Twilight Conclave as soon as possible."

"It is scheduled in less than twenty-four hours. Her concerns can't wait?"

"I guess not. She requested a conference call for you and William to discuss the matter. Perhaps your fledgling can rest while you deal with clan business."

"Can I see my daughter?" I asked.

Cass moved closer to me. "Rene, I don't see why she shouldn't see her family, provided she feeds properly first. Do you?"

Rene's fingers curled on my back for a moment before he relaxed. "Yes. She should visit her daughter."

Cass made a shooing motion with her fingers. "Everyone out. I wish to continue Raven's education."

Rene turned and exited without another word, but Dimitri looked like he wanted to murder the death dealer on the spot. "You won't be under Rene's protection forever, Cassara."

She smiled sweetly at the clan leader. "You're right, but at that moment, I will be dead. Full dead. Unlike you, I will be loyal until my heart burns in my chest."

Dimitri snarled, exposing his fangs, before he turned abruptly and stormed from the room. The slam of the door made me jump.

Cass grabbed the glass of blood she had offered me the first time. "If you're serious about seeing Jana, then you need to drink this. The choice is yours."

My fingers wrapped around the glass, and I closed my eyes before I placed it on my lips and gulped it down. Of course, it tasted like heaven, but I gagged, knowing what it was. "Happy now."

Cass rolled her eyes. "Hardly, but Dimitri will be a prissy little bitch for the next two hours, so I'd rather be anywhere but in the mansion."

I tried not to smile, but Cass never failed to surprise me with her sense of humor. "Then how about a drag club?"

"What?"

"My daughter has a room there. She works at the club." I wasn't sure I wanted to divulge my strange past yet, but nothing would stop me from seeing Jana.

Cass rubbed her hands together. "I have never been to Club Spice. Let's check it out."

I followed her from the room and avoided the multiple stares from the other clan members as we exited the building. Cassara jumped into her SUV, which had been retrieved from the restaurant as Rene requested. She was smiling when I put my seatbelt on. "Don't get too excited. The majority of the men at Club Spice are gay."

She laughed. "Actually, I assumed they all were."

"No. The club is surprisingly diverse and there are always family members who come to see the girls. Ben's brother

Leon attends regularly with his wife to support Ginger Bytes."

I had driven to Club Spice so many times I could do it in my sleep. This was the first time I ever felt nervous. The club was a haven for me as much as it was for Jana and while I believed neither Isra nor Jana would turn their back on me, there was just the tiniest insecurity that I was wrong. My thoughts continued to spiral as we drove, and my body was tense when Cass pulled into the parking lot of the club.

It wasn't as busy on the weekdays, but the club opened every night except Sundays. We stared at the sign with a logo of a spice bottle surrounded by fairy lights. I jumped when my car door clicked.

CHAPTER 19

Cass unlocked my door, using the controls on her side. From the outside, Club Spice looked like any other nightclub. On the weekend there would be people waiting outside the main doors to be led in, but there were only a couple of men smoking outside as Isra didn't allow it in the club. The two yellow-marked taxi pickups and drop-offs were empty, but it was early for patrons to leave, even on a weekday.

The large bouncer, Isra employed to manage the door and check IDs, was standing in a tight mesh top that accented every thick muscle.

Cass motioned to the bouncer. "What's his preference?"

"Darcy is bisexual."

Cass arched an eyebrow. "So you are telling me there is a chance?"

"I suppose I am."

Cass got out of the vehicle and waited for me to follow. "Do you know what the best thing about being bisexual is?"

"You double your chances of a date every night," I said

before we both laughed. "Honey, I practically grew up with drag queens."

"Sounds like fun," Cass said.

"Hi, Darcy," I said as we approached.

"Hey, Raven," he said politely, but his gaze roamed over the slick, skintight leather covering Cassara's body. While her outfit would stick out in a mundane club, she would fit right in with the various styles inside Club Spice. "Who is your friend?"

"This is Cass... Cassara."

Cass winked at him. "Cass is fine. We are on a girls' night out."

Darcy smiled. "As gorgeous as you are, you won't find a lot of takers here tonight. But if you find yourself lonely later, I get off at two and can guarantee you will by three."

Cass extended her fangs and curled her tongue around them coyly. "Careful now. You may want to ask what gets a girl like me off first."

Darcy's jaw dropped before he snapped it shut. "I have never been with a vampire." His voice was a mix of fear, and anticipation.

Cass patted his chest as we walked by. "I am willing to pop your cherry, babe. Just call the mansion and ask for Cassara. We can set something up."

We stopped just inside as the strobe lights flickered around the room. They were in between sets, so the music was louder than usual. I leaned toward Cass. "You are terrible. Darcy wasn't sure if he should sleep with you or run."

Cass smiled. "I know. Sometimes being a vampire is actually fun."

I laughed as I took in my surroundings. While there was a small dancing area, the majority of the patrons came to see the shows, so the floor area was mostly tables that allowed an excellent line of sight to the colorful stage.

There was still a long bar on one side of the room with barstools and scantily-clad waiters. The young men wore boy shorts and tank tops that displayed their ripped abdomens. Many college girls came in for the eye candy, but none of them would get lucky with the employees who worked as servers.

The bartender waved at me. Jake had been working for Isra for over ten years. He had taken the job when he was fired from his last one and needed the money, but he'd stayed because Isra treated him and his family so well. His wife came here often to visit and watch the shows.

Bottles of booze lined the mirrored wall behind Jake. While he placed a lime wedge in a multicolored drink he'd created, he poured a beer and put it on a tray before one of the servers grabbed it. He proceeded to wipe down the area where he had created the fruity concoction.

I tapped Cassara's wrist. "Isra isn't down here. He must be upstairs with Jana."

Cass glanced up. "The club has a second level. Where is the access?"

"It isn't for the club. Isra lives on the second floor. He converted it to a penthouse when he bought the building."

I led her to the set of stairs on the side that were marked with a plaque that read private. But I'd taken this route hundreds of times in the past and pressed the bar to the door and waited for Cass to come through before I released it. My boots stopped on the cement stairs as I rushed to the top, not realizing how much I had missed my family.

The door was locked, which was unusual. Isra didn't get people bothering him and they would bang on the door if needed. I knocked for the first time since I met Isra, because my keys were in my purse at the store.

"Not now!" Isra yelled through the door.

"Honey, it's me."

Isra yanked the door open. His puffy red eyes roamed over me. "Raven, is it really you? There have been conflicting reports, but neither Jana nor I believed you survived a vampire attack. We thought you were dead."

This was beyond awkward. "I did die, Isra, and nobody can explain why I transitioned... may I come in?"

He pulled me into his arms. "How could you ask me that? I wouldn't care if you were a goddamn ghost. You would always be welcome in my home."

I buried my head in his pink satin robe. I didn't realize how much I needed to hear that until he said it. "Is Jana here?"

"Of course." He glanced at Cass. "Who is your friend? She has an amazing body."

I laughed. "She does, but you have to fight Darcy for her."

Isra huffed. "As if. Darcy would break me in half, and your beautiful vampire sidekick isn't my type." He waved us forward. "Come in."

Cass winked at him. "Too bad you're a looker."

Isra took my hand and led me to the front room. Jana was curled up on the white fur couch with pink zebra striped pillows. Her eyes were even puffier than Isra's and she stared at the wall in silence.

"Honey?" I asked quietly.

Jana's eyes moved to me, and her lips parted before a squeak exited them. "Are you real?"

"Yes, babe. You know me. I have never been one to follow the rules."

Her gaze moved to Cassara. "She is a death dealer. Wait... you are a vampire?"

I nodded. "Looks like."

She burst from the couch and ran to me before jumping into my arms. Her legs wrapped around me like she used to do when she was a child. There was no way my human body could have absorbed the impact of her excitement, but I barely moved when she jumped on me and I held her as if she were no heavier than she had been at five years old. "Oh, my god."

I waited for her crying to subside, but I knew happy tears when I heard them. She took a few minutes to get control of her emotions before she allowed her legs to fall to the ground and she stepped away. She stared at Cass for a few seconds. "Did you save her?"

Cass smiled at my daughter. "I am her mentor and in charge of her safety. I guarantee no harm will come to your mother. The overseer has..." She didn't get to finish as Jana hugged her tightly.

Cass blinked as if she were unused to hugging and patted my daughter on the back awkwardly. "There. There." Yup, I definitely had to work on my death dealer's human skills.

I winked at Isra. "So what do think of the new me?"

Isra held both my arms out so he could inspect my outfit. "Prada looks good on you."

"The vamps have high-end tastes. My new wardrobe cost more than my car."

Isra pulled me against his body before Jana joined us. This was my family, and I never wanted that to change.

Jana looked up at him. "Dad, we need to get whatever supplies Mom needs for when she stays over."

Cass raised her hand. "Dad?"

Jana laughed. "Mom hasn't told you about them yet?"

Cass looked paler than usual when her finger moved between me and Isra. "You are still together."

Jana shook her head. "Not since the day I was born."

"Okay. Does someone want to fill a confused vamp in?"

Jana laughed. "I like her."

Isra released me and Jana and went to the nearby counter to pour himself a scotch. The dark skin of his hairless chest was exposed by the slack in his robe. "Raven is the female love of my life. It was twenty-one years ago. I was with a man for three years and he left me for a lawyer a week before Raven's fiancé was killed in a car accident. We had been friends since middle school and I already loved her, but in our shared anguish, our relationship turned physical."

Cass glanced at Jana. "And Raven got pregnant."

Isra nodded. "Only a month after we were together. I thought I had won the lottery. A gay man in that era does not expect the gift of children and I love Raven with all my heart. Watching her belly grow and those months we spent as a couple are still some of the happiest of my life. I will cherish them till I take my last breath."

Cass frowned. "You clearly love each other... like a lot. Can I ask why you split up?"

Isra stared at me as I moved to his side. "She is extraordinary, and I could never have been faithful to any woman... except her."

I touched his cheek. "That would never have been fair to you."

He took my knuckles and kissed them. "The night Jana was born, she told me she loved me and that we would raise our daughter together. I cried on Jana's baby blanket because the mother of my child loved me enough to let me go. She gave me everything and continues to do so to this day. Make no mistake, death dealer, I love my family and will do anything to protect them. I do not care what Raven is as long as she remains my best friend and Jana's mother."

Cass was silent for some time. "Family is important to us, but I won't lie and say this situation isn't... unique."

Isra smiled. "We made a choice to be the best parents and friends. I love her even more now than the night she gave birth to my daughter."

Jana smiled at us with unfettered devotion. "Everyone envies me. My parents never fight... well, except when it comes to fashion, and they dote on one another. They are worse than teenagers at times."

Isra and I laughed. It was true. The night I had set Isra free had hurt. It was the right thing to do, but I did love him and had he been straight, there was no doubt we would have stayed together. He had helped me get over Rodney's death when I was too young to process such a trauma. Then he gave me Jana and although I had had relationships over the years, none could compare to my love for my daughter and Isra.

Looking back, the chances of my young marriage working out were slim, but Rodney had been a kind young man, and he didn't deserve the fate that night had in store for him.

Isra kissed my forehead before Cass turned abruptly. Her hand went to her silver staff, but nobody else in the suite knew how deadly that wand was.

Rene stepped from the shadows of the room, and I glanced at the door, wondering how he had entered. "What is going on here? This is not Raven's home."

I patted Isra's chest. "Isra is my best friend. He is also Jana's father."

Rene's eyes moved over the colorful furnishings before moving back to Isra. "I see."

Jana stared at Rene. "Is it me, or is this guy super hot?"

Isra nodded. "I am secretly hoping he is gay."

They both stared at Rene like he was a juicy side of beef, and I covered my eyes with my hand. "He is the overseer, and he isn't into... anyone."

Jana sucked in a breath. "That's the vampire observer? How come nobody mentioned he looks like a Calvin Klein underwear model?"

Cass grunted before Rene shot her a disapproving look.

"I try to stay out of the public eye," Rene said.

I huffed. "Whatever. Why are you here? You are like a bad penny and keep turning up when I least expect it."

Cass stared at Rene. "I am really glad I lived long enough to see this."

I had no idea what she was talking about, but I wanted to spend time with my daughter and Isra. "Does he chase every fledgling around like this?"

Cass laughed. "Honey, he hasn't even met many of them."

Rene straightened his perfect suit. "You are easily amused, Cassara. But we must leave. The high priestess has convinced the human delegate to convene the Twilight Conclave early."

My heart fluttered. "Why?"

Rene's gaze narrowed on me. "You know why."

CHAPTER 20

It was difficult to decide which was worse. The tingling sensation beneath my skin as Rene focused his intense glare on me. Or the adoring faces of both Isra and Jana as they openly stared at the vampire overseer. It took all my willpower to turn to Cass. "Can he just walk around like this? Shouldn't he have a bodyguard or something?

Cassara laughed until I crossed my arms, giving her a dirty look. "Oh, you're serious. Yeah, that would be a no."

Isra ran his fingers over the smooth skin of his neck. I'd seen him do it many times when he was interested in a man. I was well-versed in his flirting cues. "It's a shame you have to leave, Mr. Overseer. I would have offered you a drink."

I closed my eyes and swore under my breath. "He only drinks one thing."

Isra chuckled. "Honey, do you really think I have never been to a blood club? I was young once. If you tell me an adolescent gay man hasn't tried it, I will tell you he is lying." I didn't think there was anything about Isra I didn't know. But my daughter pulled me from my shock.

"Dad, stop flirting with the overseer. He isn't your type," Jana said in a chiding voice.

Isra chuckled. "Normally I can tell after a man says a few words, but he is... unreadable."

Cass touched one of the silk scarves hanging by the door. She looked interested in the fabric, but my body went on alert when she spoke. "Jana, sweetie, how did you know Rene is not your father's type?"

Jana continued to stare at Rene. "My dad isn't the parent he is interested in."

Rene turned to look at my daughter, and she flinched under his stare. "You are observant for one so young, Miss St. Clare."

Jana glanced at Isra. "I go by my father's last name. It's Nassir."

Isra tightened his pink robe. "Raven loved my mother, and us having Jana helped my parents come to an agreement about their gay son. She wanted Jana to have the name Nassir."

Isra sighed deeply as he stared at Rene. "You sure you aren't bi-curious?"

Jana rolled her eyes. "Don't mind my dad. I swear he thinks he is still twenty-five."

"Honey, I am far more talented now than when..."

Jana popped one hip out. "Stop it. You are being rude to our guest." She turned back to Rene. "Sorry, but in his defense, you are pretty hot."

I threw my hand in the air. "You aren't helping. His ego is the size of Texas by now. He is completely unmanageable as it is."

Cassara was suddenly very interested in those scarves, but her shoulders shook a little.

Jana shrugged and winked at Rene. The overseer's lip

twitched a little, and he almost looked amused. Everybody was enjoying this byplay except me.

Rene held his hand out to my daughter. "I must tell you what a pleasure it was to meet you. I may need to enlist your help later."

Jana took his hand in rapt fascination. "For what?"

Rene winked at her. "To make your mother see my many virtues."

My daughter's laughter was like a spring rain. Her neck tilted up like a flower reaching for the sun. "I like him."

While Cass was on the verge of cackling like a schoolgirl, my shoulders sagged. "So, not helping."

Cassara cleared her throat. "In case I forget later, Raven. You are officially my favorite vampire."

Rene patted Jana's hand before releasing it. "As much as I have enjoyed this family reunion, we must go."

I hugged Isra and Jana and promised to contact them soon. Isra assured me I could come and go anytime and would have a keypad installed so he could give me the code. Cass didn't look too pleased about his admission, but she remained quiet, and we exited the door and descended the steps. The music pounded as we reached the bottom. Isra had the floor soundproofed, so the music was barely perceptible upstairs, but the thick steel door wasn't as effective.

Rene opened the door, and the bright lights of the stage refracted the hundreds of diamonds dripping from Poppy Tart's red satin dress. She twirled around the stage on nine-inch platforms while lip-synching to "It's Raining Men". His gaze moved around the club as if he were seeing it for the first time. "Interesting."

"Was it still in between sets when you came up?" I asked as I followed him to the front door. With everyone's eyes on Poppy, they didn't notice our exit.

"I don't know," he said before he opened the door for me.

Darcy puffed out his chest when he saw Rene. "Wow," the muscular bouncer whispered. He glanced at Cassara. "Is there any chance we can have a..."

Cass moved so fast that I didn't track her movements. One moment she was behind me; the next she was up against Darcy with his head pulled down close to her mouth. "Any three-way that includes two of the three vampires before you will end badly for you."

Darcy glanced at Raven. "Nobody in this club would proposition Raven."

Cass released him. "Why?"

"Isra has strict rules about her. She is off-limits for casual sex. At least if you want to step foot in this club."

I tossed my hands in the air. "No wonder I have such a pathetic dating life. Every guy I meet practically runs from me. Everybody knows Isra." I crossed my arms. "I will be having a long talk with your boss Darcy. Make sure you inform him of this little conversation and remind him I have fangs now."

Darcy's eyes moved over me. "They look good on you."

I touched the pointed teeth with the tip of my tongue, not realizing they had extended in my anger. "Damn it. I'm like a prepubescent boy."

Rene moved his lips to my ear. "I assure you there is nothing manly about you, and any man that touches you will not enjoy the wrath they incur."

"We are not talking about my dating life right now," I hissed.

Cass released Darcy. "Okay, lover. I'm willing to play with you, but the overseer and Raven are off-limits. Make sure everyone else at the club knows the rules."

Darcy looked her over slowly and it was obvious he liked what he saw. "Are you sure you can handle me?"

Cass laughed. "Honey, I could break you in half." She walked to the SUV, then glanced around. "Rene, where is your limo?"

Rene guided me to Cassara's car. "I did not utilize my driver. We will take your vehicle to the Twilight Conclave. The limo will be there to retrieve us when we are done."

Cass jumped into the driver's seat as Rene opened the back door. I wanted to sit in the front with her, but decided not to rile the overseer, considering our destination and I would be the main topic of conversation.

Rene slid into the seat beside me and draped his arm around my shoulders. "The human delegate and high priestess are already waiting for us."

Cass pulled from the parking lot as I attempted to put some distance between me and Rene.

My attempt to shove him over in his seat yielded no results, and I sagged into my seat. "I think you're far too used to getting your way."

Rene's eyes dropped to my lips, and my stomach did a little flip. "I suppose it's a byproduct of my position. I must warn you that the conclave may force me to take your blood again."

My hand slipped to my neck. "No way, vampinator. Keep your fangs to yourself."

Cass chuckled. "Have I mentioned how much I love this woman?"

Rene's lip twitched and there was a spark in his eyes that hadn't existed before. As if somewhere inside him, a light that had been extinguished long ago was slowly being reactivated. "She has a certain appeal."

I held my finger up. "No biting."

Cass laughed so hard I thought she would drive off the road. "My god Raven. You sound like you are disciplining a puppy."

I snorted. "I wish. At least you could put a dog in its pen when it misbehaves." My remark only made Cassara laugh harder and Rene's eyes flicker.

"Do not mind my youngest child, Raven. She is easily amused, but she is loyal and fairly adept at her job," Rene said casually.

Cass pretended to scratch her forehead with her middle finger, and I chuckled at her antics. "Child?"

Cass sighed. "He sired me, so I have to live with that moniker for the rest of my life. It's supposed to be a great honor and all, but you see what I deal with." While she was attempting to sound like she was hard done by, I could hear the love and affection in her voice.

I tapped my lips with my knuckle. "Yes, I can see that."

Rene shifted in his seat slightly. "I may have made an error in pairing you two."

I smacked his stomach, but he grabbed my hand before I could pull it away. "I am not accepting another mentor."

Cass chuckled. "He is fucking with you, Raven. Rene, would never trust anyone else with your welfare except me."

"Sorry. He doesn't strike me as the teasing type."

"He has a sense of humor. It's just very... dusty," Cass said.

Rene arched his eyebrow. "You ladies realize that I am sitting right here?"

I fiddled with the locket on my chest. "Would you rather us talk about you behind your back instead?"

Cass slapped the steering wheel. "Best day ever."

Rene smiled. And if I had a heartbeat, it would have stopped right there. Cass took that moment to glance back in the mirror and she sucked in her breath as Rene stared at me. "Keep your eyes on the road, Cassara. I don't have time to change my suit if you roll this vehicle, too."

Cass growled. "One time, Rene. That was one time. And it was fifty years ago. It wasn't my fault the mechanic was drunk and forgot to fix the brakes." She mumbled something under her breath as the trees blurred by.

"Where are we going? I heard the Twilight Conclave location is kept a secret?" I asked.

Rene ran a finger over my neck absently, and I tried not to react to his touch. "It changes every year and is hosted by a different faction. This year it is the witches' turn, so it will be somewhere on coven-owned lands. It gives Ursula some liberties she would not have if it were ours or the humans' turn to host. The priestess is being particularly difficult this year."

I grunted. "She needs to get laid more."

"I am going to put that on a T-shirt and send it to her," Cass said.

I put my hand to the window as we passed the sign on the road I had passed every day growing up. "We are going to the covenstead."

"Yes. Ursula has built a new meeting place on the property," Rene said.

"I heard about that, but I have never seen it. My parents always took me directly to the witch school. I have never been to the academy. That's invite-only, and I wasn't."

"You keep inferring you have little power, though that repellent magic you used on Ursula was anything but."

I dropped my hand from the window and sagged in my seat. "I never had magic like that when I was alive, so don't ask me to explain it."

Rene straightened his tie as we pulled up to a large ornate

building. I hadn't noticed his suit had silver quality when we were back at Isra's. My mind had been on the awkward family dynamic. The exterior floodlights seemed to pick up the subtle metallic threads in Rene's suit, and I glanced down at my clothes. They were the nicest I had ever worn, and I still felt out of place. "Why do you gotta be all fancy-pants all the time? I am wearing Prada and look like a hobo next to you."

Cass got out of the driver's seat quickly as Rene shook his head. "You look beautiful. My personal shopper, or concierge if you will, orders my suits and outfits my suites."

"Suites? How many do you have?"

"One at each Shadow Clan residence."

Cass opened the door. "So, Sir Fancy Pants. Do you need me inside for this?"

Rene stepped out of the limo and held his hand out for me as I followed. "Cassara, you have not been this disrespectful since you were a fledgling."

Cass shrugged. "I guess Raven is wearing off on me."

Rene shook his head. "I really should separate you."

"Nobody will protect her like I will."

Rene inclined his head. "True."

Cass winked at me. "And I wouldn't find Isaac for you."

Rene's eyes narrowed. "You know where he is?"

"I have a pretty good idea. I was thinking of taking Raven on a scouting mission."

"Why?"

Cass smiled at me. "I think she would make an excellent death dealer."

CHAPTER 21

Rene's eyes flickered. "Surely you jest? Raven will not be a death dealer."

I pulled my hand from his. "You don't think I can do it?"

The muscle in Rene's jaw ticked, as he gave Cassara a deadly look. "It's not that. Every fledgling may choose their own path. If you wish to accompany Cassara on a scouting expedition, you may. As long as the squad is with you, and you report to me before Isaac is apprehended."

Cass leaned against the rear door of her black SUV. "There are lots of advantages to being a death dealer. We have our own set of rules and even the clan heads can't interfere with us as we report directly to Rene. I am an excellent teacher, and we could use someone with your skills."

"You are referring to her magic? She isn't sanctioned to use that in the field. We would need the conclave's approval, and that is unlikely."

The breeze filtered through Cassara's pixie-cut black hair and the soft floodlight from the building at the end of the walkway illuminated her creamy perfect skin. "If she petitions to use protective magic, what is the harm? She hasn't displayed anything that could be considered a weapon. That blast repelled, but it didn't hurt anyone."

"That magic could have hurt a human," Rene insisted.

Cass crossed her arms. "Witches use magic in public all the time. Technically, she is already sanctioned to perform magic."

Rene rubbed his chin. "We will have to speak with the representatives. It may come to a vote." He held his elbow out. "Let's go, Raven. Cass can head back to the mansion. She needs to feed. My driver will return us when the meeting is adjourned."

Cass walked to the driver's door and opened it, but she leaned on the vehicle. "Be careful, I don't trust that high bitch."

I glanced back at her. "You meant witch, right?"

"Nope," she said and got into her vehicle before slamming the door.

"I really like her," I whispered as my gaze moved over the newest addition to the covenstead.

The massive new building was a log cabin and while there were new plants surrounding the wrap-around deck, there were remnants of wood shavings on the ground and the smell of cedar was prominent in the air. Though I wasn't sure if that was my vampire senses or my human ones.

The horizontally stacked logs were carefully notched and interlocked at the corners. The rich colors created and warm and inviting façade while I knew the owner was anything but.

The cobblestone pathway that led from the parking lot to the stairs leading onto the veranda had flecks of a shiny mineral within the stone. Most witches would relish an invitation to the conclave. It was a symbol of status and prestige, but I would have given anything to avoid the upcoming confrontation.

"I won't allow anything to happen to you," Rene said.

"That obvious, huh?"

We passed a rhododendron bush with pink flowers before ascending the steps. Rene paused at the door. "They are already here. Are you ready?"

"As I will ever be."

He pushed open the massive oak door, and we stepped inside.

Ursula was seated at the head of a long wooden table in the center of the large main room. Brigid sat to her left while William and his aide sat across from her.

The roof of the log cabin had a steep pitch and featured dormer windows, which added to the architectural effect and allowed additional light into the large room. Even those that surrounded the lower floor were strategically placed to enhance the scenic view.

Ursula stood from her chair and motioned to the seats beside Brigid. "Rene, please have a seat. We have much to discuss. I appreciate you bringing Raven, so we may determine the best course of action."

Rene led me to the end of the table. "There is no course of action, Ursula. Raven is mine. Anyone who attempts to harm her has perpetrated an act of war. Not only is she a vampire, but she is my personal fledgling. I claimed her while you were on the phone with me. You know what that means."

William narrowed his eyes at the high priestess. "What kind of game are you trying to play, Ursula? Raven has not done anything to prove she is a threat. Nobody has tried to turn a witch in hundreds of years. You admit she had little power. Perhaps the element in her blood that allows you to create magic was too low to poison her."

Ursula was wearing her black robe, as was Brigid. Her fingers thrummed on the polished wooden table. "I would have assumed that had she not displayed more power in death than she ever possessed in life."

William turned to me. "Raven, is that true?"

I placed my fingers on the back of the chair in front of me. "Yes, Will. I seem to have a bit more power now than I did prior to my transition."

Brigid leaned over the table. "You will address him as Delegate Francis. His is a position of respect. Even a vampire should have some decorum."

Will slapped his hand on the table. "Do I look like some pencil-neck paper pusher? I was a PSO leader before getting roped into this bull shit position. My wife was a customer of Raven's for years. I have known many people over the years who transitioned, and their personalities didn't change, provided they made it through the first few weeks. She can call me whatever she likes. You, on the other hand, can continue to call me Delegate Francis."

Ursula looked shocked. "You said you were not a fan of the overseer."

William ran his hand over his bald head. "That's right. I have been bitten by a dozen snakes in the jungle during my Seal days and those vipers had more personality than he does, but I know Raven. If you are here to propose any restrictions on her that you wouldn't on any other vampire, then this meeting is over."

Ursula glanced at Brigid, and whatever the high priestess had planned wasn't going the way she had hoped. Did she honestly think that Will would side with her because I was a witch? "I wasn't suggesting we hurt Raven. I think we need to put restrictions on her use of magic. That power belongs to the coven and should not be utilized by... Vampires."

William grunted. "Are you kidding me? She was a witch. Just because she was the first to transition doesn't mean she will be the last. I don't know if there's any way to test her blood now, to figure out what makes her unique, but I am guessing Rene is already investigating that."

Rene inclined his head toward the human delegate. "I am. We wish to know if Raven is unique or if other witches can petition to enter our ranks."

Ursula stood up abruptly. "Shut your mouth. No respecting witch would want to become a vampire. Raven was attacked. She would never have chosen this. Ask her."

William rubbed his forehead. "Of course she wouldn't have. Until she transitioned every witch assumed it was a death sentence. Hell, this could be a fluke accident or something else. We won't know for another few hundred years. Either way, that doesn't make her a monster." He flicked his hand to Rene. "No more than him, anyway."

Ursula smoothed the front of her robe and sat down. "I apologize for my outburst, Rene. Since none of us have any idea of what Raven's evolution should be or if she will survive the initial phase of her transition, I recommend we limit her use of magic."

William leaned on the oak table. "Raven, what kind of magic do you possess now? Still growing plants?"

"No, Will. When Ursula attacked me in the limo, I created a protective... blast to repel her. So far, my magic has been reactive to attack only."

Will turned to Ursula. "You tried to kill her?"

"Not kill her. Immobilize her. The public is not safe with her on the streets. Not in this condition. She must be culled."

Rene's growl was low, and William looked more shocked than the high priestess and Brigid. "This meeting is over. I will not tolerate threats to any of my people, especially my own fledgling."

Will stood and raised his hand. "Let's calm down. Rene, please have a seat. Raven you too." His voice was calm, but his eyes remained glued to Rene. When the tall vampire didn't move, he turned to me. "Please, Raven."

CHAPTER 22

I wanted to appease William. I respected him, but I felt like I was a duck out of water, with my spidey sense warning me I was in danger.

The head priestess looked up as William pleaded with me. Her gaze locked with mine and her smile was wicked as candles on the wall sconces ignited around us. I hadn't noticed the wrought iron holders when we entered, but they had very specific placing around the room, and I was sure they enhanced the bearers' powers. Ursula's power. "Come in, my sisters," she said before the door in the corner opened and a dozen black-robed witches entered the room. They moved to stand behind Brigid, and the second-in-command of the coven smiled at the human delegate as his gaze roamed over the coven members now in attendance. I felt the energy building around me, but couldn't identify the source. With so many witches in the room, it was impossible to single out the threat.

"What is the meaning of this, Ursula?" William asked. It wasn't against the conclave's rules to invite others to attend.

My presence was requested after all, but Ursula had invited her coven seniors. All of them.

The priestess lifted a silver pendant she wore around her neck. I'd seen it hundreds of times but assumed it was an heirloom. The enchanted talisman began to glow as she whispered words under her breath. It had to be some kind of incantation, but it wasn't one I was familiar with. I heard her call to the elements to protect the living and the surrounding building and I formed the protection spell in my mind, making sure it encompassed both me and Rene. I strengthened the invisible bubble when I felt the pendant's connection to the witch's form. Ursula was siphoning from the witches around her and if she needed that much power, it wasn't good for anyone in the room. I could feel the priestess' desire to rain fire down on the vampires in the room.

William must have realized her plans for Rene and me would end with us as piles of ash because he slammed his fist on the table. "Whatever you are doing, stop it. I will not tolerate an attack during a Twilight Conclave."

Ursula remained focused on her enchantment, but she flicked her hand, and the coven began to circle the table. A witch approached me with her hood over her head and while she looked to be about my daughter's age, I didn't recognize her. Her wrist flicked toward me before a lightning bolt bounced off my shield. While neither Rene nor I were singed, the impact made me stumble and a barrier spell formed between us. It forced me backward into the corner, and while I knew the witches would kill Rene if they could, there was no doubt who the true target was. Only three of the black-robed figures stayed with Rene. The rest moved to stand in a semi-circle around me.

While I focused my shield on two witches advancing on me, it left my side open, and another slipped in and stabbed me in the back while I was trying to repel her sisters. It cut off my power and shield at the same time and forced me backward as I fought for my life. I almost cried with relief when Rene called my name. He was whirling between bolts of energy, but he kept bumping into an invisible shield between us. My steps were faltering, and I needed blood to replace the quart I had left on the floor. After focusing on my protections, I managed to grab the hilt of the dagger embedded in my lower back and yanked it out with a shriek of anger and pain.

My arms flew up and a bolt of energy shot from my hands and hit a witch in the shoulder, thrusting her backward until she crumpled to the floor, groaning in anguish. I didn't have time to enjoy my small victory, as the rest had resumed their attack on my weakening shield.

I felt the tissue on my back and shoulder attempting to heal, but I needed blood to speed the process. I sent a pulse of power into the wounded area, and while the infusion of magic helped, it wasn't a replacement for vampire nourishment. Rene continued to growl, and the low vibration from his throat made the hair on my neck rise. He fought like a pissed-off gladiator, though I could only track his movements when he encountered the barrier spell that kept me from him.

William continued to scream at the witches, and his fist banged against an invisible shield. The coven had three separate bubbles erected to ensure we couldn't band together or help one another. I had no idea what Ursula was thinking. If Rene or I died, she would be guilty of treason and the coven disbanded or handed over to another territory. Ursula was the current matriarch of all the covens, but she still had to abide by conclave rules. The fate of the lycans was a reminder of what happened if you alienated the humans. They didn't need to side with you. They just had to ignore you and let the supernaturals fight it out. Once they sided against you. It was over as it was for the werewolves. A witch broke through my shield and launched herself at me, but my power erupted like a bolt of lightning, and she slammed into the log wall beside us with a resounding crack before crumpling to the floor.

I left the witch to writhe on the floor and started fighting my way toward the head priestess. The level of energy building around us matched the pulsing light in the room. The priestess took the glowing pendant and placed it at the center of the table. The wall sconces surrounding us flared once more. That made it the focal point of her growing energy. I felt it pull some of my magic, but concentrated on the source. Panic set in as I erected protective barriers around my core of power. That weakened my protections, and another dagger found its way into my side as William screeched at the witches.

I was torn between attacking the priestess so I could stop her from unleashing her spell and keeping my intestines inside my body. I lurched forward, clutching my side, when I noticed Ursula raise her arms in the air. A beam of light arced from her palms to the pendant as she directed more energy toward it. Was she planning on unleashing a magical bomb? If she dropped the protection shield, Rene and I would be incinerated. My heart was pounding so hard against my rib cage that I was certain it was going to be a bruised mess in seconds.

The head priestess called out to the elements with her arms raised in the air. A witch didn't typically call on this power while inside a building. Energy sparked between her fingers, and I felt a storm brewing within the room. Rene growled, splitting my concentration. He was dodging a lightning rod when I looked over. There was a charred piece of fabric hanging from his chest, and his suit jacket was on the floor in a heap. His fangs flashed as his red eyes tracked the witches surrounding him. But when he attempted to get to me, he hit an invisible shield and bounced off.

Ignoring the witch lobbing balls of flame in my direction was difficult, but I had to concentrate on the protection spell I had erected. The orange light was bright enough to illuminate the entire room, as if we were standing under the midday sun. William continued to shout and threaten Ursula with death, war, and other unpleasant repercussions, but she seemed oblivious to his threats as she continued to harness the building power. My invisible protection saved me when a laser of energy pierced the bubble and hit my shoulder. Had it not been in place, I would have been incinerated on the spot, but the beam lacked the power to spread to my heart and I moved from its deadly ray while my skin charred in a circular pattern. I had never experienced such pain, not even when I was hungry, and I had to focus as crimson tears flowed down my cheeks and crackling energy formed in my palm.

The front door burst open and a squad of PSO officers burst into the room with their weapons raised. While they held their specialized rifles up and moved into formation, they equipped their black vests with UV lasers and various other weapons. The squad leader unclipped a vial and tossed it on the table. It shattered against the wood, and the pendant began to sizzle and hiss when the strong liquid came in contact with it. Ursula swayed in the air before she seemed to snap to her senses. The PSO officers were running up against the same barrier Rene was, but with so many bodies in the room, it was only a matter of time before they diagnosed the source and took out the witches responsible. Witches had to share magical repellants with the human delegate, and Ursula was running out of time before her force of witches fell.

Ursula moved toward me, and her black-robed members moved to allow her to pass. Rene was joined by several PSO officers, and they were attempting to remove the remaining shield between the coven and them. My former high priestess stopped as she encountered my now-weak protection. "I could smash this, but I wish to talk to you, Raven."

I clutched the wound at my side and blood flowed between my fingers. "If you wanted to speak to me, we would have had the conclave. This was an assassination attempt. You want the vampires dead."

"I have no love for the undead, but they are not the target. You are."

"You hate me that much?" I whispered.

"Not you. What you represent. You are the blood witch and the prophecy about you has circled the coven for fifteen hundred years. Honestly, I believed it was an old wives' tale that the witch who transitioned all those years ago was a myth. But here you are, and the most powerful monster in the world is protecting you. I cannot allow an abomination like you to ruin the supernatural world."

"What is the blood witch? What are you talking about?"

Ursula raised her hands. "You don't need the details. Just know that your death ensures our future." Lightning cracked between her fingers before it slammed against my shield, breaking it like glass as magical shards exploded around me.

CHAPTER 23

The power that erupted from inside me wasn't a soft ripple over a still pond. It was a volcano that exploded from my core like a supernova, and I slumped to the ground as Ursula hurtled backward. The witches lost their grasp on the shield that acted at a barrier between them and the PSO officers and William barked orders to subdue the coven and take them into custody as Rene scooped me into his arms.

The chaos reigned around me but my eyes closed and all I could focus on was the warm scent of Rene's neck next to my lips. I nuzzled his skin as my fangs sprouted from my gums.

"You never cease to surprise me, little bird. How am I supposed to keep you safe?" His voice was low and with the shouting between the witches and the PSO squad, it was hard to focus on his words.

As much as my body hurt and my hunger beat at me like a wounded animal, my mind shied away from the reality of what I needed. "No," I croaked as if the words were wrenched from my soul.

"So defiant. Even now, when your body burns with the

need to appease your hunger and mend its damaged tissue. Is the thought of feeding from me so repugnant?" his voice held a hint of self-loathing. Maybe it was regret. Rene was difficult to read at the best of times, and I was in no condition to trust my instincts.

"Not you..." There was more I had wanted to say, but my train of thought was replaced by searing pain in my stomach as the need to feed overshadowed the desire for my body to repair itself. Maybe it was the same thing. I curled into a ball in Rene's arms.

"Please, Raven, take sustenance. I have shielded you from the others, and William is busy arguing with the priestess. This will not end soon enough for us to return to the mansion."

The thought of the ride home under these circumstances was daunting, and I had to accept there was no syringe in my future. "Not the neck." That was way too personal, and I needed to put some distance between me and the sexy overseer. While my mind shied away from the reality, my body was more than down for some biting. And it wasn't necessarily confined to his upper body.

Rene extended his pinky fingernail and made a small incision on his chest. As soon as his blood welled on the cut, my lips clamped over the wound, and I moaned lightly. The spicy scent was nothing compared to the vibrant flavor that burst on my tongue. I had tried the bottled blood and though Cass had assured me it was the best quality, it was nothing compared to the euphoria on my tongue, courtesy of Rene.

His body froze as his arms tightened on me slightly. Not enough to hurt me, but enough to remind me of the strength of the predator that held me. And inform me he had no intention of letting me go. As I snuggled closer to him and the pain inside my stomach eased, I could feel the tissue on my side and back meld together. The overseer's blood was highly effective and just as addictive, and he was forced to move my lips from his skin by inserting his fingers between them.

"That is enough, Raven. The human delegate will need to talk to us. Tell me you are up for it."

My tongue slipped over my lips, and I tried not to focus on my behavior. I didn't think I would have stopped if Rene hadn't interfered, and that was downright scary. What if I had fed on a human? My daughter. Isra. "Yes," I whispered, but my guilt laced every word.

"Raven, your hunger is expected. A fledgling should never be exposed to this kind of violence or injury. I failed to protect you and I will not make the same mistake again."

My eyes lifted to meet his, and my heart flipped in my chest. While his words were soft and comforting, his eyes blazed like crimson beacons. His anger pulsed below the surface, and I touched his cheek tentatively. "This isn't your fault. You can't protect me from magic, and I had no idea Ursula would risk a confrontation with the PSO. She has put the entire coven at risk, and I won't be surprised if they replaced her as the coven matriarch. She may lose her status as high priestess of the Black Blossom Coven as well."

The glow of his eyes subsided as I spoke to him, but he moved his jaw over my hand. "Your power is greater than I expected."

I moved slightly and Rene reluctantly placed me on my feet, but he continued to use his body to block me from the commotion behind us. "I never possessed power like this. I can't call on the power to encourage plant growth, but I can call on a magical energy wave or protective shield. I can't explain it."

We both turned when William called my name.

"Raven, can you join us?" I wasn't sure he had seen Rene

feed me, but he likely knew what was going on. He had to have seen the dagger in my back before I could remove it.

Rene put his hand on my lower back and led me toward the long table. The priestess had her hands tied behind her back and sat at the head chair where she had started her power spell. "Raven will survive, no thanks to the witch betrayer."

Ursula hissed. "I did not betray anyone. Least of all my coven, or the humans. Raven is the blood witch. If she is allowed to live everything we have worked for will be for nothing. This world will be laid to waste."

"Another apocalypse prophecy."

Ursula huffed. "Not for you, but for the rest of us."

I moved closer to Rene. "I would never hurt anybody."

She stared at me with unveiled contempt. "You don't understand. You can't deny your hunger. No vampire can. Your destiny is written, and you can't be allowed to fulfill it."

William motioned to the leader of the squad, who had subdued the rest of the coven. The two injured witches had already been removed on stretchers. "Remand the coven to the holding cells. They were acting on Ursula's orders, and she will be held responsible for their actions, but none of them may attend a Twilight Conclave for the remainder of their lives."

Brigid hissed as she struggled with her bindings. "You can't do that. We followed the instruction of our elder."

William put his hands on his hips. "Which is why you will not be charged, but not one of you will become the next high priestess as she is required to attend the conclave. Every one of you has screwed your career and I think there is a good chance you went along with this insane plan so Ursula would be incarcerated. That would have made you the next coven leader, wouldn't it, Brigid?"

Brigid spit at William's feet. "We follow our high priestess out of loyalty. The blood witch will destroy us."

William flicked his wrist. "Take them out. I have had enough of their hypocrisy." He turned to Rene. "I must apologize. I never thought Ursula would be this brazen. We will question her together in an attempt to have full transparency in this investigation. I promise this will be sorted and the source of this prophecy discovered. We will not allow such behavior from any faction."

While William had effectively apologized, he had also managed to warn Rene that they would not tolerate any retaliation for her attack.

Rene inclined his head. He looked regal despite the singed remnants of his shirt, which left the majority of his spectacular chest exposed. "I take public safety very seriously, William. I assure you nobody in my clan will retaliate for the high priestess' action or they will deal directly with me."

William stared at Rene for a few seconds. "That little death dealer of yours is a powder keg. She is going to go apeshit when she learns you were attacked."

"I will ensure Cassara keeps her knives to herself."

William glanced at the door as the remainder of the witches were led out of the building in cuffs. "We both know she doesn't need a knife."

Rene shrugged. "That is true. I am quite proud of her skills."

William turned back to Ursula. "Tell me about this blood witch prophecy."

Ursula stared at me. "I don't know all the details. There are five pages to the prophecy, and all are located in the dark flower. But I possess only one."

"Black Blossom County," I whispered.

Rene was like a statue. "You will share the page your coven possesses, and we will search for the rest. I promise to disclose anything we find to the coven and to William."

"I don't trust you, vampire," she hissed.

William leaned close to Ursula. "He could have killed your entire coven once that protection spell fell. You will hand over the page or your life. I am done with your antics, Ursula. You will be given time to find replacements for your coven and assign a new matriarch, but your days as head priestess are over."

Ursula turned to him. "I don't care about my position. I care about the survival of my species. Every witch alive will back me once they know the truth."

"Had Raven or Rene died, we would be at war, and make no mistake, you don't have the numbers to win. I am sure the vampires would stand aside if we asked them to, and honestly, we don't need their help to annihilate you."

Ursula sucked in a breath. "How could you hate us that much? We do everything we can to help the humans."

"We both know that is a lie, Ursula. Anything you do for us is to ensure your species thrives." There was a whip to his voice, and I wondered what the high priestess had done to make an enemy of the new delegate.

She glanced at Rene. "You would stand with them? The bloodsuckers?"

"We would have to. We stand by the accords we created to end the last war. Tell me we are united in our cause."

The priestess glanced at me. "I would rather die."

Rene growled low. "That can be arranged."

CHAPTER 24

"Back off, Rene," William snapped. His cheeks were red, and I knew his anger wasn't aimed at the vampire overseer. His tone softened. "Take Raven home. I want to have a private chat with the high priestess."

Rene turned on his heels, taking me with him. There were only two PSO officers left within the new covenstead building and neither of them was Cameron. I had no idea if he had been part of the team that had escorted the witches to their holding facility for processing. In all the confusion, I hadn't checked, but he hadn't approached me, and the team rotated days off. God, I hoped he had missed this assassination attempt. He would hear about it though, and I expected a text from him soon.

Rene removed his shirt once we were outside and tossed it in a bin full of cut branches and a few broken tiles near the entrance. It left his athletic upper torso bare, but he had ripped the tattered cloth from his body as if it was offensive, and I had to admit the smell of charred cotton was unpleasant when you had heightened senses.

The limo was waiting for us at the end of the pathway and as we neared it, a vampire in a black suit with a black pin-stripped tie rushed to open the rear passenger door for us. He glanced at Rene's lack of shirt with concern. "I did not bring a change of clothes, sir."

Rene flicked his hand as he waited for me to enter the limo. "We are heading home. Alert the clan that the high priestess attacked me and Raven. No coven representative is to be trusted until further notice."

The driver hissed. "I will contact Dimitri on the way back. Your supply is stocked, and I will have you home shortly."

Rene followed me into the back seat. The leather didn't make a sound as he sat beside me, but had creaked when I slid in. Rene fitter than me, but he towered over me, and his form bordered on muscular. He was far more toned than I had first imagined and I found it difficult not to stare at his abdomen. I had seen Greek statues with less definition.

When the driver returned to the front seat and the partition between us was raised, it emphasized the silence of the night, and the events of the last hour became very real. My own coven had tried to kill me. I had never felt so alone or betrayed. I may not have been a powerful witch, but I knew some of the ladies standing behind Ursula. They had been regular customers in the store. While Ursula's betrayal hadn't shocked me, I didn't expect their entire coven to vote for my death. My fingers slipped over both eyes before the first sob racked my body.

Rene pulled me into his lap and kissed my forehead. "I am sorry, Raven. These people are not your family. I don't believe they ever were. They follow their leader blindly."

His scent was as comforting as his words. "Your people follow you, too."

Rene moved his lips to my ear. "Do you believe Cassara would kill an innocent without proof? Has she not told you her story?"

I thought about Cassara's human life. Working behind the scenes to help women in need. She had said she investigated her targets to make sure the men she planned to assassinate warranted the kill. "Not when she was human. But doesn't she have to follow your orders?"

"She questions my orders frequently. She is my senior death dealer and I do confide in her in most matters. I value her input and trust her like no other."

I laid my head against his chest. "I'm glad you have her." My body sagged in his arms.

Rene tipped my chin up. "I am as well. Training her seemed essential to the longevity of the clan. There were moments when I almost enjoyed it."

He was trying to tell me something. His eyes searched mine, but I was too broken to discern his meaning. "Okay."

"I know about betrayal, Raven."

"Did everybody you grew up with vote to kill you, then line up to do it?" A red tear slipped from my eyes and Rene leaned down to kiss it from my cheek. How had I ended up here? Turned on by the people I trusted and comforted by the most powerful vampire alive.

"Not all of them," his lips moved to the corner of my lips and before I could ask what had happened, they connected with mine.

His touch was soft, sure, and passionate. My mind blanked out as our mouths moved against one another and his tongue slipped between the seam of mine. The events at the covenstead blurred in the back of my mind before my body began to tingle and I pulled away.

What was I doing? Was that me or him? This was wrong

on so many levels, but while my mind was sorting through the reasons I should stop him, my gaze roamed his perfect body. My fangs extended, and I covered my mouth with my hand before Rene pulled it away. "I don't think this is a good idea."

Rene looked almost amused. "May I ask why?"

"Cass said you don't... date. I'm not a casual relationship kinda girl. We don't even know if I will survive the first few weeks. Why put yourself through that?"

"I admit I haven't been interested in a woman in over a thousand years, but even those dalliances were meaningless."

Yeah, that made sense. I would be horny after a thousand-year abstinence, too. It had to be the circumstances. Rene identified with my predicament in some way. That was all. Having reasoned out his interest in me, I pulled farther from him.

"You fear me. Why?"

"No, I don't," I said too quickly. Liar. Liar. Pants on fire. The overseer wouldn't break my heart. He would snap it like a dry twig. No woman could compete with him when it came to sexiness and a freak of nature witch sure wouldn't keep his attention for long. Hell, he rarely cared about anything. He would simply return to his usual emotionless state. And I wasn't a once-every-thousand-years kinda girl.

"Raven," he chided. Yeah, his bullshit meter was probably at ten, but what did he expect?

"Look. You are... well, you. And I am... well me."

Rene was silent for some time. "Was that vague response supposed to convey something? I am aware of what you are."

I had thought battling the coven was bad. His apparent interest in me had wiped my melancholy away, but only because I had no idea how to deal with this situation. "I am a phase. Probably because I'm a witch. Like a shiny new toy or something. You will tire of me soon, and that isn't for me. I will do my best to integrate, and I will be loyal to you, but I can't be what you need."

His arm moved to the seat behind me. "And how would you know what I need? What I want? You are too busy running from me to take the opportunity to get to know me. Rene Roth. Not the overseer of the vampires."

I grunted. "I am right here. And I haven't run from you."

Rene moved like a jungle cat. The muscles in his stomach flexed slightly, and I found it difficult to rip my gaze from his chest. "You run from me emotionally."

My jaw dropped. "Are you kidding me right now? You have the warmth of an ice cube. You barely get irritated, let alone laugh. No offense, but I prefer my men to be a little more responsive."

He moved so fast that I didn't have time to react. One moment he was lounging in the seat next to me and the next he had his arm around my back and me pressed against his body. He held me gently, but I was caged in his arms. "I think you will find I can be quite responsive when provoked."

I swallowed hard. "I wasn't trying to provoke you."

"Yet you did, nonetheless."

"How?"

His eyes flickered. "You died. You are a miracle."

I shook my head. "I'm a mistake."

CHAPTER 25

Rene didn't answer me, but his disapproving look said it all. The driver pulled up to the front of the mansion and it seemed like the drive had taken only seconds, but that was likely because the overseer had effectively distracted me. He opened the door and stepped out before holding his hand out to me.

With his sexy, shirtless body, I felt like a princess being led to the castle. There were a few vampires standing near the fountain, and they all stared at Rene as he held his arm out to me. I must look like an insane woman leading her arm candy to a pool convention instead of a mansion and I kept my eyes down to avoid the stares prickling the back of my neck.

Fortunately, Rene didn't pause in the foyer and led me through the throng of vampires and up the stairs before Dimitri stopped us on the mid-level landing.

Dimitri's eyes roamed over Rene's upper torso. "Were you hurt?"

"No. But my attire did not survive the witch's fire. Have you informed the other clans about the attack?" Rene asked.

Dimitri's lips thinned as he smoothed his red tie. "Not yet."

"Inform the other clan leaders immediately. Ursula is the current matriarch. They will have to deal with the repercussions of her actions."

"She is in custody, then?" Dimitri asked.

Rene glanced at the throng of vampires gathering at the bottom of the stairs. They were likely waiting for the overseer to address them after learning about the attack. "No. There are... Stipulations. Her reign is limited while they start the process of replacing her and the Black Blossom Coven. I must attend to Raven. They injured her in the attack." He didn't wait for a reply. He simply led me up the second staircase and continued silently until we reached his private suite. Once inside, his tense shoulders seemed to relax. "Would you like a shower before you get changed?"

I picked at my ruined clothing. "You have no idea how much."

Rene began unbuckling his leather belt before my hand shot out. "Alone. I want to shower by myself."

His lip twitched, and I dashed to the bathroom and slammed the door before leaning against it. What happened to my life? Sure, I wasn't the most conventional woman when it came to choices, but dear god. How had my life become so insane?

I stared at the massive white marble tub with envy, but made my way to the stand-up shower. The matching double sink and beveled mirror were like any other bathroom. The missing toilet was the only thing that screamed vampire. After turning on the hot water, I removed my clothes and boots before depositing them in the empty garbage bin. Like everything else in Rene's life, the bathroom was uncluttered. It was the complete opposite of mine at home.

Between Jana and me, our bathroom looked like a fairy garden of colorful brushes, make-up compacts, and scrunchies. Then there were the various shampoos, conditioners, and soaps. If I had three square inches of free space, I'd be surprised. This bathroom had nothing but a bar of soap beside the luxurious crystal tap.

I tested the water and found it a little hot, so I added a bit of cold and stepped in. There was a single bottle of shampoo, and it held the faint smell of mint. It was better than nothing and I used it on my body and my hair. After rinsing the long strands, I stepped from the shower and grabbed a fluffy white towel before wrapping it around me like a sarong. It reminded me of my stint in the morgue and my mind shied away from the memories.

Rene was leaning against the wall in just his pants, but they were undone, and he no longer had socks or shoes on. "I will have a quick shower while you get dressed."

I didn't trust my voice as the thought of him naked sent a shiver down my spine and I was trying to forget the kiss from earlier. No man should be able to kiss like that, no matter his species. There were at least a dozen new additions to the walk-in closet, and they were all on my side. Had Cass added to my collection or was Rene's personal shopper expanding my wardrobe with Rene's? My heart flipped when I saw the newly-tailored red jacket. It was stunning, with several pockets and gold accents. Grabbing a simple white blouse and black pants, I dressed quickly.

There were several more pairs of black boots, similar to the ones I had worn earlier, but those had joined my clothes in the trash. The bedroom was lavish and had two large dressers in it, but I couldn't find a brush.

I turned when Rene exited the bathroom, wearing only a towel around his middle. While he had been sexy shirtless, his skin glistened as he ran his hand through his wet hair. I had to turn away before I drooled like an idiot on his floor. He went to the closet as I tried to figure out what I should do next. There was a slithering in my stomach, and I closed my eyes briefly, trying to wish the hunger away. I tried to focus on the sound of the hangers moving in the closet and the sound of a belt being done up. When Rene exited, he wore a new pair of dress pants and held a shirt in one hand. As soon as he saw me, he tossed the shirt on the bed.

His eyes flickered red as he approached me. "Raven, you need to feed."

"We can go to the feeding room. Maybe Cass will give me another syringe, just until..."

Rene put his hands on either side of my face. "I have never begged another to feed from me, but I will for you. Please trust me. I will not allow you to do more than seek nourishment. I want our first time together to be without the influence of my venom."

If my stomach weren't turning on itself, I would have taken more time to contemplate his words. As if our union was only a matter of time. His lips met mine with the softest of touches. It was sexy, but I could tell that wasn't what he wanted. He needed me to feed from him. As if my trust were the most important thing in the world to him.

Pain was an impressive motivator and while my mind shied from the thought of biting him, my body was urging me to do just that. My lips moved over his chin, and I nipped him once as his muscles tensed. The scent of fresh mint mixed with his unique scent and my tongue took a cursory lick of his skin as I made my way to the base of his neck. He grunted and his hand tightened on my waist as my fangs lengthened.

I nuzzled him several times and when he groaned my name, I realized whatever I was doing was like vampire catnip. Every tendon in his body was pulled tight and his erection pressed against my stomach.

"Caramia, please," he whispered into my ear. He growled low when my fangs pierced his vein, and I drew his life-giving fluid into my body.

He tasted like passion and spring water. And I pressed into him as if I could hide in the shelter of his body. I'd never had a reaction like that to any man. Not even Isra and I loved him more than any man I had dated later. The hunger evaporated, and this time, I made a conscious effort to swirl my tongue over the wound. It closed, and I forced myself to step away.

We were both aroused, and I took several breaths, hoping it would calm the firestorm in my veins while Rene walked to the bed and grabbed his shirt aggressively. Blue balls were a bitch no matter who you were, and I took solace in knowing he wasn't immune to a feminine touch. As long as it was mine.

Shit. I couldn't think like that. He couldn't be mine. He was the fricking overseer and likely had hundreds of women vying for his attention. "Thank you, Rene."

He kept his back to me as he slipped on his dress shirt. "The pleasure was mine, Raven. Do you feel better?" His tone had returned to that emotionless void that made me shiver, and not in a good way.

"Yeah, but I am really going to miss chocolate."

Rene moved to one of the dressers and opened the top drawer. "I had Cassara contact your daughter. She was quite forthcoming about your likes and dislikes." He took a chocolate bar out of the drawer and handed it to me. "You will retain your taste buds for at least another fifty to a hundred years. There are no dietary advantages, but most fledglings enjoy the sensation and taste."

I took the gold bar and ripped off the wrapper. The rich chocolate melted on my tongue, and I moaned. "Thank god."

Rene looked like he was about to say something, but he turned and glanced at the door before there was a loud knock.

"Rene, open up. There has been an attack," Cassara yelled through the door.

Rene opened his front door, and she walked in. "Why didn't you use the adjacent door?"

Cass flicked her hand to his bare chest. "Because I have no desire to see your balls out. Raven is welcome in my suite whenever she wants, but you still have to knock."

Rene stared at her as I stifled a laugh. "Tell me about the attack. Was it the witches?"

Cass glanced at me. "I have no idea. We have seen nothing like this before. The team is checking the archives to see if there is anything like this in our history."

"Who was killed, and how did they die?" Rene asked.

"It was Alexander. He looks like someone dipped him in cement," she said.

Rene's eyes flickered. "They turned him to stone."

Cassara's eyes narrowed on her leader. "Is that even possible? Have you seen it before?"

"Not personally, but I've heard of one other such attack. We need to investigate. I want to see Alexander's body for myself."

Cass turned. "Raven, do you want to come to the car with me while Rene gets ready?" I jumped to follow her, and we were in the hallway, closing the door to Rene's suite in seconds.

"Balls out?" I asked with a chuckle.

Cass winked at me. "I like to make sure Rene doesn't let his power go to his head."

"There is no chance of that with you around."

"You say the nicest things," she said in a flirtatious manner.

We descended the stairs to the murmur of voices in the foyer. Almost every pair of eyes moved to me, and many of them were belligerent in nature. Cass put her hand on the silver staff clipped to her belt.

"I am pissed I didn't enter the conclave with you and Rene. Part of me is hoping someone will attack you again so I can take out my frustration," she said it loud enough for every vampire in the room to hear, and I pursed my lips as the majority of them looked away.

Our boots clicked on the tile floor as we walked beneath the massive crystal chandelier, but I felt safe next to Cass, and considering the night I'd had, that was awfully strange.

"Allow me," Rene said as we approached the door.

I startled and grabbed Cassara's arm. "Dammit. How does he move so fast? If he keeps that up, we will have to put a bell around his neck."

Cass burst out laughing as Rene moved ahead of us to open the door. "Man, I would pay good money to see that."

Rene arched an eyebrow at his death dealer. "You are far too easily amused."

I smiled at Rene. "I would have to agree with her."

He shook his head as if he were being mistreated, but his lip twitched at the side. He followed us outside and the driver opened the rear door to the limo to allow us entry. Cassara sat opposite of me, and Rene took up his position beside me, slipping his arm around my shoulders. I was getting far too comfortable with the vampire overseer and his penchant for keeping physical contact with me. "Where was Alexander found?" he asked.

Cass rapped on the glass partition, and it rolled down. "Take us to one-forty-one Lemur Road."

"That is only a few blocks from my house," I said.

"A mundane home. Why was he there?" Rene asked.

Cass leaned against the far door. "They were having a toga party. A few of our clan members were in attendance, but the majority of the partygoers were human. The owner of the house is a mundane woman named Lisa. She is quite distraught, and William's people don't think she's involved."

Rene nodded. "If she isn't a witch then it is unlikely. But it can't be a coincidence that one of our people died the same night that Raven was attacked."

"You were both targeted. Your death would ensure a war, but I doubt the human is involved."

My shoulders jolted as the limo came to a stop and the door opened. Rene exited first and held his hand out to me before we were standing in front of a massive home with white patio lanterns strewn across the lawn and patio. It was peaceful and beautiful, as were the manicured bushes with solar lights lining the walkway.

Rene stared at the large home. "Let's see this vampire statue."

CHAPTER 26

We ascended the steps and although we knew this was a mundane home and there were only humans on scene, Cass walked ahead of us with her hand on her silver staff. Her squad was in a black van behind us, and they filed out, moving to the bushes to surround the building as we entered the open brass double doors.

The entrance to the large home was brightly lit with an array of Christmas lights wrapped around the banister that led upstairs past the various picture frames. The faux wreaths and draped sheets added to the Roman feel. It looked like the kind of party Isra would enjoy and since this had been a mundane home with predominantly human guests, I felt bad that it had ended on such a morbid note.

A PSO officer in full black tactical exited one of the rooms from the hallway in front of us. He clicked the mic at his neck. "They are here. I will bring them in." He motioned us forward. "He is in here. I apologize for bringing you out so soon after Ursula's treachery, but we have no idea what this is. It took us some time to realize he was one of yours."

I recognized the man from the covenstead. He was

leading the PSO team members who apprehended the witches and took them to holding. I had no idea where the PSO prison was, and I didn't want to. It was rumored to be underground and the thought of that was any witch's worst nightmare. Of course, I wasn't like any other witch. Not anymore.

"Thank you," Rene said, and the officer nodded and popped back into the room.

We passed several pictures of a woman in her late thirties with two elderly parents and several of her growing up. I assumed the woman was the owner of the house and she smiled in every photo.

Cass entered the room ahead of us, and my gaze moved to the statue lying on the bed. Had he been standing up, I would think someone had removed him from the Greek wing of the Seattle museum. His skin was slightly cracked, and his eyes stared open at the ceiling. His toga looked more like something you would get at a costume store than one from ancient times, but it still added to the overall effect.

The bedroom itself had a single bed and one dresser. The small closet was closed and with only a picture of a dog and a candle on top, I assumed this was a guest room. Family bedrooms would be upstairs, though I was unsure if vampires stayed in town during the daylight hours.

"Do not touch the body. We will have it remanded to the city morgue for testing," Rene said.

Cass knelt down beside the bed. "Not that I am against a reason to cozy up to that sexy mortician, but why aren't we taking responsibility for our clan mate?"

"I have no idea what caused this, but Derek will probably have to cut into the body with a saw. I don't want any particles transferring to the clan until we know how this... thing is transmitted."

Cass backed away. "Are we in any danger?"

"There are reports on the last time this happened, and I believe it is safe while the body is undisturbed. Other vampires were around the previous victim of this disease and nobody else was infected. I believe it came from an outside source, but it was never determined."

The PSO officer stayed close to the door, but there were a series of static clicks before he swore under his breath. "We have an issue at the prison. Cass, I am releasing the scene to you and pulling my team. I will notify Derek on the way out that you wish him to carry out the testing on this."

Cass nodded. "Thanks Murdoch. I appreciate you calling me."

Murdoch's gaze lingered on her. "No problem." He exited the room, and his mic clicked again. "Move out. Death dealers have the scene."

Two vehicles started in the distance before their engines faded away.

I was about to ask Rene more about this strange vampire illness when both Cass and Rene hissed. "What is it?"

Cass bolted past me. And glanced out the door into the hallway. She already had her silver staff in her hand, but she hadn't extended it. "We are under attack. They must have been waiting for the PSO team to leave. They are attacking my squad with blood darts. Most of the team is down. How did they get their hands on those, Rene?"

Rene growled. "We will do an inventory of the clan weapon rooms upon our return. There must have been a theft. Even I am not immune, but I can purge the poison from my system quicker than you can."

Cass glanced at me. "What effect will it have on a fledgling? Nobody except you has seen these in use."

"It could kill her. We must ensure they do not inject her."

There was a crashing sound at the front door. "You might

as well come out, Raven. I know you are here. The death dealers are having a nap. Rene overworks those poor bastards," Isaac laughed at his own joke.

Cass stepped from the room, so she was facing the vampire who killed me as Rene and I followed. They were shoulder to shoulder, and I had to peek around them to get a look at my attacker. "You have some nerve showing up here, Isaac. Why did you sell out your own people?"

Isaac growled. "Rene sold us out a long time ago. I'm simply righting a wrong."

"You care nothing about politics, Isaac. You want power, but you are unwilling to work for it. How many times were you turned down for council duties at your former clan? It's ten now, isn't it?"

Isaac kicked an unconscious death dealer at his feet. "No matter. There will be a new world order and none of you will be part of it."

Cass clicked the button on her staff, and her spear extended. "I think you overestimate your skills."

There were shouts from outside as Isaac turned. "Looks like the death dealers are waking. I didn't want any witnesses for this job. They will effectively take out the mundane mercs I hired to distract them, but I wanted to keep things fair, so I outfitted them with UV bombs."

There was a flash in the night and a blood-curdling scream. Isaac laughed. "Hand Raven over and I won't pump you and Rene full of Dark Dahlia.

"Never going to happen, asshole," Cass said as she moved in front of us.

Isaac raised a small crossbow with six red darts, ready to be released. "I was hoping you would say that."

The magic that bubbled from my core was not like that at the covenstead. It arced around me like a snow globe, glittering as Isaac pulled the trigger. The dart embedded in the glowing orb before he shot another.

"No!" he yelled, before pumping off two more rounds.

I could feel the darts pressing against the outer shield as if my barrier was hindering them but not stopping them. "We're going to have to move. When I drop the protection bubble, they are going to continue their journey." The darts moved in a circular motion slowly, as if they were on a rotisserie.

Rene stepped closer to one. "What kind of magic is this?"

"I have no idea, but we don't have a lot of time." I could already feel the magic fading inside me, and I focused on the bamboo plant in a large ceramic pot close to me. While using the power to create the strange bubble, I couldn't locate the thread of magic that connected with the roots of the foliage.

Isaac dropped the small crossbow and grabbed a thin flashlight. "Let's see how you like UV rays. You all need to work on your tan." He clicked on the laser-like beam, and it reflected off the protective bubble, but I flinched as the stress of maintaining it increased.

Rene touched my shoulder gently. "Move to the side so the darts don't hit you and drop the shield. Isaac is a traitor and the mundanes are helping him. If they make it into the house, we will be outnumbered."

While I had to agree with him. There was no way I could maintain this field for much longer. There was no way I would survive a UV laser.

"Trust me," Rene said softly.

Cass turned sideways at the same time I did, so we were both out of the line of sight of the twirling darts. I recalled my magic and the bubble dropped as the darts sailed past us and embedded in the wall at the end of the hallway. The laser light flashed toward me and while I ducked, it caught me in the shoulder and I screamed as my flesh seared. I was covered by Cassara's body a split second before there was a gust of wind and everything went silent.

Cass moved and helped me to my feet before checking the charred remains of my shoulder. "You'll heal." When she turned toward the empty door, I saw the massive burn on her back. The skin was already knitting together, but the material of her suit had been burned away, revealing how powerful that laser had been.

"Oh, Cass," I whispered.

She grabbed my arm. "It's nothing. We need to find Rene."

"Where is he?"

"Chasing the traitor."

"He is faster and stronger than Isaac," I said confidently.

"Normally, I would agree with you." She pointed at the empty dart on the floor.

CHAPTER 27

Cassara and I bolted through the doors to find Rene holding Isaac by the throat. With his victim's back against his chest, he was next to a manicured bush that looked like a poodle. While the vampire overseer could easily hold his own with the undead traitor, a man in black tactical gear similar to that worn by the PSO was standing ten feet away, with a rifle aimed at Rene's head. There was no doubt in my mind that the gun contained another blood dart, and Isaac held another in his hand, ready to jam it into the overseer's leg.

Several death dealers stood in a semicircle around the trio of men, and I wondered why they were hesitating until I noticed the dart embedded in Rene's chest. It hadn't taken him down yet, but that was his second dose of dark Dahlia, then the one in the rifle or the one in Isaac's hand would.

Cass made a small gesture with her hand and the death dealers backed away, blending into the surrounding bushes. "Give it up, Mark."

The man holding the rifle curled his lip. "It's not going to happen, bloodsucker. The PSO sold out to the vampires. At least the witches are human."

"Every vampire that walks the earth was born human."

Mark kept his rifle aimed at Rene and Isaac. "You are a disease. One that should have been wiped out centuries ago. But that mistake is going to be rectified."

"Shoot him," Isaac shouted at Mark.

Cass snorted. "Obviously you weren't listening, Isaac. Mark probably sought you out. He wanted a chance at Rene. That dart in his gun has more than dark Dahlia in it. He is waiting for Rene to kill you. Isn't that right, Mark?"

Mark grunted. "The only good vampire is a dead vampire. And by dead, I mean a pile of ash at my feet."

"You prick!" Isaac shouted.

Mark motioned to Rene. "Go ahead, kill him. I will even answer one question for you before you join him," Mark said.

Long claws extended from his fingers and curved into needle-like points. I'd never seen or heard of any vampire being able to shift or alter their physiology in some way. By the look on Mark's face, he was just as surprised.

Isaac raised the dart in his hand slightly, as if he planned to stab Rene with it, but the claws around his throat were not the ones he should have watched out for. A bloody hand burst from Isaac's chest, and I was reminded of an alien movie until he dropped the heart on the ground.

Isaac's mouth moved before he slid from Rene's grasp and fell to the dirt. The whisper of wind was slight before Mark's rifle fell to earth beside Isaac and Mark was being hoisted in the air by Rene.

"Don't kill him," Cass shouted as she rushed toward the enraged vampire overseer.

His cheekbones were ultra defined and the death dealers approached from the surrounding shrubbery with caution as he ripped the loose dart from his shoulder. The skeletal look and animal-like claws were obviously new to everyone in the front yard... except Cass. Her eyes were on Mark.

Mark spit on the ground when Rene lowered him to his feet. "It doesn't matter if you kill me. This is only the beginning, bloodsucker. Your species is on the brink of extinction. You just don't know it yet."

"You know him," Rene said in a gravelly voice that sounded like he was in his own personal wind tunnel.

Cass nodded. "He used to be a member of the PSO. William fired him for breaking protocol. He tortured a few of our brethren. They were innocent of the crimes Mark accused them of."

"No vampire is innocent," Mark snapped before he grabbed a small globe at his belt.

Rene made a quick flick of his wrist and Mark's neck snapped like a small twig beneath his fingers. "Cass, call William. Inform him of his former employee's activities. Neither Mark nor Isaac were the instigators of such an elaborate plan and neither is capable of creating a potion that will turn a vampire to stone."

Cass grabbed her cell phone as Rene bent down and bit into Mark's neck. He took several gulps before moving to Isaac's body and repeating the process. His eyes were like red lasers in the night when he stood, and a cracking sound echoed before Cassara turned to him. "Rene!"

Rene moved his neck unnaturally to the side before his overt features dissolved and his claws retracted. "I am fine, Cassara, but we are under attack."

I glanced around the clearing at the clearly wary death dealers. "From who?"

Rene shook his head. "Not here. All vampires are under attack. Isaac was commissioned to kill Raven and her daughter, but he didn't know who hired him. Mark was part of a secret organization. They shield their faces from one another, but most communications were done via the internet."

Cass stared at Mark's body. "Isaac was some kind of vamp mercenary? Why would he turn on his people?"

Rene turned to me. "That is the question, isn't it?"

"What does that mean?" I asked.

Rene's eyes flickered. "We are at war."

Find out what happens next in the Magical Midlife Death series by reading Forty Proof and Dead.

Continue reading for a preview.

FORTY PROOF AND DEAD
CHAPTER 1

*R*ene grabbed my arm and pulled me closer to him. "Cassara, have your team secure the area and have Isaac's body returned to the clan morgue." I stared at the body with a hole in the center of his chest. While many humans still believed the myth about vampires turning to ash when they died, that was only true if they died as a result of UV exposure, and the older the vampire, the slower the process. Rene could smolder for hours before the sun's rays hit his heart. Cooking like a rotisserie chicken was a gruesome way to die, and I planned to avoid it at all costs.

I stumbled slightly when Rene led me to the black limo. The breeze moved through Rene's hair, highlighting his features, but the hand that had taken Isaac's heart was still visible in the moonlight. It was covered in dark blood that also stained his shirt and jacket.

While it looked like I was getting into the luxurious car with an axe murderer, he had been protecting me. How much pain and controversy had I wrought with my transition? Rene barely had time to concentrate on clan issues, and his responsibilities were not confined to the Shadow Bone Clan. I didn't even know how many shadow clans there were. Only that Cassara had created the newest one in Quebec City.

I took the seat Cassara normally did across from where Rene typically sat. While I would never tell him that his current appearance was offputting, considering he had executed one of his own to ensure my safety, I needed a reprieve. He took his usual seat and crossed his legs casually, as if he didn't notice the dark stains on his hand and jacket. Was murder an everyday occurrence for the overseer?

"You are nervous. Did my appearance bother you?" he asked quietly.

I motioned to his jacket "Not the clawed hand thing, but your arm looks like you were fishing for treats in a vat of blood." I answered honestly.

Rene leaned forward and pulled off his suit jacket. He folded it so that the sleeves were tucked beneath, then rolled up his shirt cuffs. After there was no trace of blood showing on the fabric, he opened the small fridge and pulled out a cloth. After he had cleaned his hands, he placed it back inside and flashed me his palms. "Better?"

"Much, but I don't have the right to complain, considering Isaac was after me. Do you have any idea why he would turn on his clan? I doubt he was working with Ursula."

The limo pulled from the driveway of the home as Rene rubbed his chin. "Isaac was a member of Shadow Skull clan. It is one of our more... temperamental factions. But they had not seen him in over a month. He did report that he was traveling to Shadow Bone and spending time with us, but he never officially checked in. Cassara is looking into his movements in the last four weeks. If she can discern where he was staying, hopefully it will give us some leads as to his agenda and conspirators."

Soft classical music played in the cab of the limousine. It

was soothing, but the hunting nature of the song reminded me that my death was only the beginning. Fate had a wicked sense of humor, and I was the center of a supernatural storm. "Do vampires commonly visit other shadow clans?"

"Yes. Travel is encouraged between the clans. It encourages unity and offers those without a partner to find one."

While I had studied vampires as part of witch school. The facts about them had been technical in nature. There had been nothing about cultural intricacies. Maybe the coven had never taken time to learn the reasons behind vampire turns or their clan values. "Is a partner so important to them?"

"It doesn't start out that way. Not unlike humans, we have an... evolution. But yes, we do seek an eternal partner, eventually."

I leaned forward. "Really?" There was no hiding the interest in my voice.

Rene smiled. "A fledgling is typically interested in the... excess our culture offers. Blood. Sex. Money. Power. But those things become hollow after some time. That's when we learn the only way to truly live is to have someone to share those sensations with."

"So, I am in my party phase?" I asked.

Rene chuckled. "I suppose you are."

"Well, I am too old for toga parties and Beer Pong." When he didn't answer, I realized that even if I wanted to, no amount of alcohol would get me drunk. Changing the subject from my ignorance seemed prudent. "After you find a permanent partner. Do you get married?"

"Yes. But it is a little different from a human ceremony." He glanced out the window as the trees passed us by. It was obvious he didn't wish to discuss the subject, and I had been through enough for one evening.

"I am really sorry about Isaac. It's unfair you had to..." I fidgeted with my hands on my lap, because I wasn't comfortable saying the word murder. Kill. "One of your own."

There was no sound or whisper of air displacement, but Rene's arms circled my shoulder before he pulled me against him. "You are not responsible for Isaac's betrayal."

I stared up at him. "We really have to talk about your sneak attacks."

His lip twitched. "Is that what they are?"

"You keep it up and I'm going to buy that bell."

He pulled me closer to him, settling my head on his chest. His chin rested on my head and he stared out the window. It was like cuddling, but lacked the quiet familiarity I felt with Isra. But I hadn't been attracted to Isra in a long time. As I inhaled Rene's unusual sandalwood scent, my skin began to tingle. I wasn't sure if he wanted me close or he felt I needed the contact. Cassara had told me that mentors tried to fill the void of human connections in the first few years. Making transition easier for a fledgling. Rene was trying to ease my concerns. It wasn't his fault I was attracted to him. Hell, who wouldn't be? It was either that or he didn't trust me, and that brought a pang to my chest. Why should I care? I didn't have an answer, but I found that I did.

"Can I ask about the other clans and interpersonal relationships?" I asked after a long pause. He seemed content with silence. Me, not so much.

"You can ask me anything, Raven. I plan to teach you everything I know."

I was sure he meant everything about being a vampire. He was an overseer and I would never have that kind of power. Nor did I want it. "Do vampires... get divorced? Do they ever tire of each other after a few hundred years?"

He was quiet for some time. "No. When a vampire takes that particular oath, they are together until death. When one partner dies, the other can decide if they want to move on or look for another. The longer they are... bonded, the harder it is to move on if there is a loss."

"It sounds kind of beautiful, actually."

Rene pulled his arm from my shoulder. "We are home. The sun is rising. Stay beneath the canopy." The limo rolled to a stop and Rene exited the vehicle, holding the door open for me as I followed. A string of color lined the horizon, and it all seemed more vibrant than it had in the past. I paused to watch as the sun crest in the distance and a prickling feeling moved over my skin. It didn't hurt and felt more like a warning or an alarm. He pressed on my back and I knew he wanted to go inside, so I allowed him to guide me through the large entrance doors.

The foyer had a few vampires chatting in the large room, but every one of them looked up as we entered, and every set of eyes followed as we made our way to the stairs. I put my hand on the railing as my legs became lethargic. Vampires always seemed to have an endless supply of energy, but I felt like I was fighting to keep my eyes open. "I feel like I ran a marathon."

"Fledglings require far more sleep than a senior vampire. You need to get some rest." We continued until we reached the hallway that led to his and Cassara's suite. My heart flipped as we passed her door and he opened his.

He began undoing his shirt as soon as we entered, and I was thankful he'd left the suit jacket in the vehicle. I was sure it would end up in the garbage and confirmed my suspicions when he threw his shirt in the trash bin beside his dresser. My eyes moved to the adjacent door that led to Cassara's suite.

I just stood in the middle of the large room like a statue,

fiddling with my hands. Rene turned to me when he realized I had remained motionless. "Is Cassara's door open?"

"Do you need to use her bathroom?" he asked.

"No. I think that crisis is over. Looks like I am like the rest of you in that department. But I assumed there was a bed for me in there."

Rene's lip twitched, and I almost told him what I thought of his amusement. He hadn't had to rely on another for a bed in a long time. Maybe never. He was probably old world money or royalty. "I will show you to your room." He led me to a hallway with two rooms. Both doors were closed, and he opened the one closet to us.

I entered the pristine room. It had a queen bed with a red bedspread and matching curtains. As well as a large vanity with a brush and some lotions or perfume. There was a closet and a black velvet chair and I wondered why my clothes were in his walk in instead of in here. It was simple, but nice. "Thank you. What is in the other room?"

"That is my office and entertainment area."

"Entertainment? As in a large-screen TV or movie theatre?" I asked with interest.

"Yes. I do have a viewing area. I believe Cassara even has a subscription to Netflix."

I laughed. "I should have seen that coming. She is a woman after my heart."

"She is not the only one," he said. The comment was so casual I wasn't sure if he meant Cameron, him, or Isra. There were so many differences between human and vampire culture that what I construed as flirting could be something completely different here.

I pointed to the vanity. "That's nice. Did Cassara pick that?"

"No. She does not spend a lot of time on her appearance.

Her focus is on the safety of her and her team. I am honestly curious what she will wear to the next vampire ball." I wasn't sure what he meant by that, but I smiled at him as my eyelids became heavy. "Get ready for bed, Raven. I will check on you shortly." He exited the room as I opened the closet.

There were a handful of silk nighties and two robes, but the rest of my clothes were in the walk-in closet in Rene's main room. It was comforting to know he watched TV. Though I hadn't seen him enter his office once since I had been here and I changed into a black nighty before pulling back the covers of the soft bed. I moaned as I slipped under the covers and fluffed my pillow. The soft cotton seemed to call to me and my eyes drooped instantly.

I was almost asleep when Rene entered my room. If I wasn't so tired, I would have drooled. He wore simple black silk pajama bottoms and no shirt. "Man, you could make a killing on the cover of those male magazines," I whispered before I realized I had said the words out loud.

He placed his hand on either side of my shoulders, though they were beneath the covers, before leaning down. "Be careful, little bird. That sounded a lot like flirting."

I sighed. "I'm too tired to flirt and you are too... you for someone like me."

He was silent for a moment. "I am sure you will explain that in more depth when you aren't on the brink of sleep," he said.

I snuggled further into my covers. "Not a chance. You are far too confident as it is."

He kissed my forehead, and my heart fluttered. It was quite a feat for something that didn't need to beat. "Good night, Raven. I look forward to tomorrow." The bed shifted slightly, but my eyes refused to open.

What happens tomorrow?

FORTY PROOF AND DEAD
CHAPTER 2

I stretched under the soft cotton sheets, then inhaled the faint smell of strawberry and tangerine before my eyes fluttered open. My hand slipped beneath my pillow before my fingertips touched the small pouch. My fingers clutched it before I pulled it out to inspect the contents. The mesh lining was filled with flecks of dried fruit mixed with various herbs. I smelled it to confirm it was the source of the faint aroma in the room. Since it was appealing, I put it back and wondered if Rene had put it there. More likely it was Cassara, but I doubted she would admit to it. My death dealer mentor was as much an enigma as the overseer.

After flipping back my covers and sitting up on the bed, I found I was completely refreshed, but had no idea what time it was due to the blacked-out windows. You could see out of them, but the dark tinting did not allow me to discern the time of day. My eyes moved around the simple room to a wooden clock mounted on the wall. I'd only been in bed for five hours, yet I felt like I had slept for twelve. Maybe vamps didn't need as much sleep as humans.

I got to my feet and went to the closet only to remember

that all my clothes were in the main walk in, so I grabbed a robe and slipped it over my shoulders before opening the door and exiting the room. My bare feet skid over the shiny wooden floor as I peeked into the main room. "Rene?"

When I noticed his bed was made and there was no activity, I went directly to the closet and began leafing through the clothes. After a few minutes, I realized there were even more outfits than there had been last time. "Damn things breed every time I turn my back." I said before clutching my chest when Cass walked into the closet.

"Hey girl, find anything good."

I dropped the blouse I had been holding. "Dammit Cass. You scared the life out of me."

She shrugged. "You're already dead, so that's not technically possible."

"Ha ha," I said and picked up the blouse off the floor.

I motioned to all the clothes. "There is a god damn closet Genie living in this place. There are more outfits every time I come back. They are all my size and most are exactly what I would wear."

Cass ran her hand over a velvet gown. "Yeah, Rene has Louis beefing up your wardrobe. He used to do it to me too, before I... spoke with him. I think that poor vamp is more afraid of me than Rene."

"You didn't like the clothes he chose? He seems to have exceptional taste," I said as I grabbed tan pants to go with the black blouse I had chosen.

"Louis has amazing taste, but he kept buying me dresses. I'm just not that girl and the slicks the death dealers wear are custom made for us. I don't need much else."

"So, there are no yoga pants in the Cassara James closet."

She grunted. "Of course there is. I don't wear my slicks for movie night."

I pulled a purple crop top from the closet that wouldn't cover my breasts. "This, on the other hand, needs a new home with someone younger and thinner."

Cass laughed. "Just throw anything you don't like on the floor and it will get returned. Are you ready to do some training?"

I turned to her with my clothes in my hands. "What kind of training?"

"I was thinking I would show you some moves. To see if you're cut out to be a death dealer. It's completely fine if it's not for you."

My heart fluttered, and my veins hummed. "I would really like that. Are the clothes I picked out okay? For training, I mean."

"You're just going to be in the training facility. They are fine. If we run, I will get you new ones. I'll wait by the door while you get dressed." She exited the closet as I pulled off my silk nightie.

I was dressed in under a minute and found my hair looked like I had just brushed it when I hadn't. There was even a slight glow to my skin, which struck me as odd considering what I was. Apparently, vamps looked good after a few hours of shuteye. After pulling on my boots, I joined Cass by the front door. She was turning out to be fun and entertaining to be around. Everything I didn't believe a vampire could be. Still, I got the impression that most people didn't see the side of her Rene, and I did. Probably her death squad teammates, but the rest of the clan looked at her with unveiled weariness.

We exited the suite and headed for the stairs. "Where is Rene?" As soon as the question left my lips, I regretted it. I had no rights in the clan as a fledgling and couldn't expect to monopolize his time. Cass wasn't his personal valet, either.

"He is meeting with William about the coven and the

repercussions of their attack on you. He won't be back for a few hours if all goes well. It gives us more time to train and get you acquainted with the team."

"I wonder what he will do to the witches who followed Ursula's orders. Her rule is absolute. It would be like a vampire going against Rene. I hope he takes that into consideration."

She grunted. "We know that, and so does William. They have been released from holding, but the PSO is monitoring their movements going forward.." We descended the stairs and found a handful of clan members in the foyer. They all seemed to meet there and then go to their prospective activities, though I had no idea what those were. The mansion was massive, and I was sure there were rooms for just about any entertainment, but I wasn't ready to join in whatever those were.

There were several well-dressed males staring at Cassara as we made our way to the hallway on the other side of the foyer, but if they glanced at me, their looks were disapproving. I ignored the overtly judgey stares as we left the foyer and entered the adjacent hallway. This one had more pictures of men in suits from another era, and none of them smiled. We passed several closed doors before Cass opened one and I followed her inside.

My jaw dropped at the sheer size of the room. The foyer was deceiving In that it acted as a hub with various hallways angling away from it. The rooms that attached to those hallways were far larger than I assumed they would be. This one was the size of a small stadium.

One wall was lined with weapons, many of which I had never seen before. That side was lined with mats and roped off areas that I assumed were the training area.

The opposite wall was split in two with a sizable room

that held a long table, chairs and audio equipment. It was likely for debriefings and presentations and beside it was an indoor shooting range. My father had been a hunter and though we had countless arguments over his activities, he had taught me to shoot a rifle by the time I was ten. I had even gone into competitions until I was sixteen. While I had loved shooting, I couldn't kill an animal up close. I had watched Bambi a hundred times as a child, and to this day, I couldn't eat venison. And had openly cried every time I had to put down a pet due to age. Animals were wary of vampires and as a witch, I assumed it was because they recognized another predator. One stronger, faster, and deadlier than them.

I stared at the large black boxes beside a tactical training area that had visibly movable rooms and apparatus. "What are those?"

"They are virtual training simulators. Man, I wish we had those when I was learning. They allow one of my members to practice combat scenarios in a controlled environment. I can adjust the program while they are in the stream. Trainees have to get a perfect score on the program before they graduate to the tactical area."

Val and Quinn were wearing only their pants as they sparred in the corner. The floor of the facility reminded me of a gym. As did the circular black tape. Both men were extremely fit and countered each other's moves. It was obvious they had done this many times before, and I pitied anyone who got in the ring with them.

"Where are the rest of your team?" I remembered there were at least a half dozen surrounding us at the house, but there had likely been more hiding in the shadows.

"They are either feeding, on clan business, or off. This is a slow time of day for the facility. Most vamps like to sleep in. We aren't usually called out until late evening hours when our brethren have had a chance to get into trouble."

"Sort of like after hours at a bar."

"Something like that." She pointed to the wall of weapons. "Pick one and I will show you some moves."

My gaze moved over the long wall with dozens and dozens of weapons mounted on it. While there were several staffs that I soon extended like Cassara's did, they weren't silver and appeared to be stainless steel instead. I chose one and pulled it from the wall. "Okay. How do I use this thing?" I was looking for a button that I assumed Cass clicked to extend it.

She took the weapon out of my hand and turned it so I could see the pattern inscribed on. The circle appeared to be part of the design, but when she pressed it, the end extended and a blunted spear burst from the top.

I took it for her and inspected the blunted weapon. "Not exactly like yours."

"We don't use lethal weapons in here. Accidents happen and a silver spear in the heart for a trainee is instant death. These hurt like a bitch, but won't kill you."

I twirled the spear in my hand, displaying far more dexterity than I had as a human.

Cass narrowed her gaze on me. "How did you do that?"

"I was a baton twirler when I was younger, but I haven't picked one up in decades. I guess it's like riding a bike."

Cass grinned. "Just when I didn't think you can get more interesting." She grabbed another of the staffs from the wall and extended it before motioning toward a black circle. "Get inside the ring. If you step out, it's a point for me."

I didn't have, and he took a stance opposite of me. "Now what?"

She held her staff loosely in both hands. "Now you attack me."

I attempted to copy the positioning of her grip and swayed the staff with the blunted spirit in the air a few times. "What if I hit you?"

The men chuckled from the other ring, and my confidence took a hit.

"Don't listen to those jerks. They both get a round in the ring with me next."

"Aw Cass," Val said, but Quinn laughed.

I swung my staff toward Cass when I thought she was distracted by her teammates. I was hoping to hit her staff, but she flicked mine so hard it tumbled from my hands. "Ouch."

Cass flexed her hands on her staff. "Make your grip look loose, and your wrists should be, but you hold on to your weapon like it is a lifeline, because trust me, it can be."

I picked up the staff and tried again, but while I managed to keep the staff in my hands, I stepped from the ring after Cass hit the center three times. "Damn Cass." The third round yielded the same result, and I sighed when it fell to the ground.

"Let's try a laser," Cass said.

"You have UV lasers?" I asked.

"Of course. If it works on a vamp, we have it." She took my staff from me and went to the wall before returning them to their clips. Then she grabbed two sleek black flashlights before returning to the ring and handing me one. I took my stance opposite of her again.

"Any tips before you hand me my ass?"

She held up the UV laser. "Grip it so the base wrestled on your shoulder. It will give you more stability until you get the hang of it. If you go up against the rogue, you shine it in his face. It doesn't kill him, but it blinds him and it's a lot easier to stab him in the heart if he doesn't see it coming."

"So you use the UV lasers to blind rather than kill."

"Keep in mind that the majority of our assignments are capture missions. Most vamps can be rehabilitated or confined to their prospective clans."

"You have vampires that are not allowed off clan property?"

"When you break clan rules, that is the most common punishment."

I moved the flashlight back and forth, getting used to the weight. "Vampire grounding. Cool."

Quinn snorted. "When she says it like that, we sound like toddlers."

I winked at him. "If the fangs fit."

Cass laughed and motioned for me to attack her. I was about to switch on my laser when the door to the facility opened and Rene walked in. My stomach did a little flip as my gaze roamed over his black suit. The man really should be on the cover of a magazine. His eyes went directly to me as I lowered my laser.

ALSO BY TIA DIDMON

Tia has written over 60 books. For a complete list and a reading order visit:

https://tiadidmon.com/book-list/

ABOUT TIA DIDMON

Tia Didmon is a USA Today bestselling author of provocative paranormal romance and paranormal women's fiction. When Tia isn't busy writing about sexy shifters and dreamy demons, she spends her time binge watching The Order and reruns of The Vampire Diaries, cooking with her daughter, and serving her cat. Her love of writing stems from a self-diagnosed book addiction.

Subscribe to Tia's newsletter at tiadidmon.com for a free book and start your journey through Tia's supernatural world today!

CONNECT WITH ME!

I love interacting with my readers. Follow me on your favorite platforms and/or message me through my website or Facebook.

Website - https://tiadidmon.com
Email – books@tiadidmon.com
Booksprout - https://booksprout.co/author/4408/tia-didmon

- facebook.com/tiadidmonauthor
- x.com/TiaDidmon
- instagram.com/tiadidmon
- bookbub.com/authors/tia-didmon
- amazon.com/author/tiadidmon
- goodreads.com/tiadidmon

Made in United States
Troutdale, OR
11/08/2024

24582477R00135